THROUGH FOREST
AND STREAM

Adventure in the Mountains

BY DUANE YARNELL

WILDSIDE PRESS

CONTENTS

CONTENTS

THROUGH FOREST
AND STREAM

1. BEAT STATE!

THE two young athletes were inseparable. Both were juniors at Tech where they had excelled in sports. One was tall, well-muscled Ted Moran, Tech's star pitcher and the son of Tech's athletic coach. The other was Bill Lawson, who, because of his short, heavy stature, was known affectionately as Pudge.

Now it was the last week of school and both boys were looking toward the coming summer. Examinations were over. The only important event on the schedule was the last baseball game of the season. The game was to be played the following afternoon against State, the new school in a near-by city.

This morning, Ted and Pudge stood in the hallway of the old, ivy-walled school. They were gazing at the trophy case their athletic feats had helped to fill. It was Pudge who opened the conversation.

"You know, Ted, summer is almost here. My folks told me yesterday that they could afford to send me to summer camp. You're still going with me, aren't you?"

Ted Moran's steady brown eyes lighted in anticipation. "I'll say I'm going. I've saved my money all year and while I haven't nearly enough, Dad has promised to supply the rest. It will be my graduation present from him—a year in advance."

"Boy!" Pudge exclaimed, "I can hardly wait. Think of it, Ted. You and I up in the mountains together, surrounded by lakes and forests and wild animals!"

Ted grinned. "I can smell the pine woods already. Say, I've got to leave you for awhile. Dad left word with my math professor that he wanted to see me. Wonder what he could want?"

"Oh, he's probably worried about the game tomorrow. But I don't know why he should be. He was a great baseball pitcher in his day and you're his son. I don't know what more a coach could want than to have his own son pitching for him."

Ted departed immediately. He walked out across the campus to the small building that housed the gymnasium. He waved a greeting to several friends as he entered, then turned into the small office to his right.

"Hi, Dad," Ted said. "You sent for me, didn't you?"

"Why . . . oh, yes, Ted. Have a seat. I'll be with you in a minute. I have a few papers to sort."

Ted Moran sat down and for the first time he noticed the frown upon his father's face. Usually Coach Moran was a friendly person. His honest face was ordinarily the location of a beaming smile. But today the Tech coach seemed strangely disturbed.

"Ted, I want to talk to you about something that may not be very pleasant. But we have to face facts, whether it's now or later."

Ted felt instant alarm. "Bad news, Dad?"

"I'm afraid so, Ted. I may as well start at the beginning. As you know, Tech is supported by state money. We're an old school, Ted, but we're also a poor one, financially. You see, we haven't been getting too much help lately—barely enough to keep the college going. To make a long story short, the athletic governing board has decided that there isn't enough interest in baseball here at Tech. So after this season they're abandoning the sport. I guess you know what that will mean for me. There won't be a job for me any longer. It's a tough blow, Ted."

Ted Moran felt the physical force of the blow as much as did his father. He forced a smile. Then he walked over behind the desk and threw his arm around his father's shoulders.

"Look, Dad, you're worrying needlessly. You're a great baseball coach. If Tech can't use you, other schools will want you. Don't take it to heart so."

The older Moran looked up at his son and for an instant, a trace of a smile flickered over the corners of his mouth. "You're loyal, Ted, but you don't know too much about the coaching situation. You see, I'm an older man. I've been here for twenty-five years. Colleges aren't hiring old coaches when they can get young ones. Besides, Tech is a small school and while we've managed to do well enough in our own league, we aren't known all over the country like other schools."

"But I don't see how they can make Tech quit playing baseball," Ted said huskily. "They aren't making State quit. State is also kept going by state funds. There's really no difference in the two schools—except that State is newer."

The coach sighed. "No—there isn't any difference, Ted. Except one thing. State has been getting more money because the men who control the money believe the new school is more popular than ours. But unfortunately there is nothing we can do about that. I work for them and I have to abide by their decisions."

"Then there's absolutely nothing we can do?" Ted asked.

For the first time Coach Moran began to show some of the fighting spirit for which he was famous. He looked up and his eyes were flashing as he said, "There's only one thing. We play State tomorrow. We aren't given a chance of winning by the sports writers. But if we beat them, we might be able to prove that Tech still likes baseball. I'm not certain, but it's possible that with a victory to our credit, I could talk the athletic governing board into extending our baseball program. It would look odd to the papers if, after we defeated State, our baseball program was scrapped and State's continued."

"My arm's in great shape, Dad. If it takes a victory over State, you can depend on my doing my share. We've got a fighting chance. What more could a Moran ask for?"

Elderly, wise-eyed Tim Moran stood up, and this time the friendly grin was back on his face. "I feel better already," he said. "But I'm keeping my fingers crossed until tomorrow."

Ted also kept his fingers crossed. He hardly slept that night, and the next day he was on edge until the game started. But after his first pitch, his nervousness vanished.

The first State batter hit a ground ball to the Tech infield. The Tech third baseman fielded the ball and threw the runner out at first.

Ted wound up and again threw his fast ball. The umpire called it a strike. In short order Ted whipped over two more strikes and the second man was out. The third State batter hoisted a short fly that the Tech first baseman caught. It was three men up and three men out.

"That's the way to scrap," Coach Moran told his boys. "Now let's see you get out there and get some runs for yourself."

But getting runs wasn't easy. State had a real ball team. Their men understood the game, and today they were playing back of a man who could pitch as well as, or better than, Ted.

Pudge was the first Tech batter. With two strikes against him, he swung desperately at a curve. The ball cracked off his bat and streaked through the infield. A fast runner could have reached second base. But Pudge Lawson was heavier than most of the men around him. He pulled up at first, panting.

From first base, Pudge shouted, "Get a hit, Ted. Drive me home with a run. We can take this State bunch."

The State first baseman was a tall, heavily built fellow. He had dark hair and a dark, scowling expression. His name was Stone and because of his rugged disposition, he was known to his mates as Rocky.

Rocky Stone said, "Don't make so much noise, fat boy. You were lucky to get this far. You won't go any farther."

But at that instant something happened that changed Rocky Stone's mind. Ted Moran, standing at the plate, had seen a fast ball coming down the line at him. With only a split second to swing, he had stepped into the pitch. There was an immediate resounding crack. The ball went far up into the sky, seemed to hang majestically against the fleecy white clouds, and then began to descend. The fans in the small Tech grandstand held their breath as the State outfielder scampered back. Then a loud cheer went up.

"It's over his head, Ted. Run! Run! Make a home run out of it. You can do it, Ted."

Ted Moran was running like the wind. He saw the ball fall far in the outfield. Ted started to round first base—and then, it happened. Ted tripped over Rocky Stone's foot and went hurtling through the air. His instinct told him that the tripping was not accidental. He had seen Rocky Stone's foot reach out, but he hadn't had time to avoid it. However, the game was too important to interrupt right then. So Ted rolled to his feet and continued to race toward second. He saw that it would be a close play. Ted left his feet and dived for the base. His fingers touched the canvas square, a split second before the State baseman put the ball on him.

"Safe!" cried the umpire. Then when Ted picked himself up off the base, dusted the dirt from his clean white uniform, the umpire moved over to him, whispered, "Too bad about your accident. You would have made a score if you hadn't fallen. I didn't see it too well—you stumbled, didn't you?"

It was not Ted Moran's way to complain. Rather than spoil the day by getting into a conflict, he said, "I . . . I stumbled. It was an accident. Perhaps I'll be luckier next time."

Instead of hindering him, the accident really helped Ted. For the very unfairness of Rocky Stone's move had so angered him that he settled down and pitched the best baseball of his career. The baseball followers in the grandstand had seen the whole thing, and they were quick to condemn. For the rest of the game, every move that Rocky Stone made was soundly booed. And Rocky, who usually played flawless ball, was so unnerved that he committed several glaring errors in the field.

Rocky Stone wasn't used to such things happening to him. And the man he blamed was Ted Moran. So a personal feud soon developed. Ted realized it would be better to ignore Rocky and thus avert trouble. This he did successfully until the first half of the ninth inning. The Tech team, playing heads-up ball, was leading by that one lone run that Pudge had made in the first inning on Ted's long hit.

"Just three more men," Pudge Lawson shouted from behind the plate. "Three more outs and the game is ours, Ted."

Out on the mound a grim-faced, tired young pitcher took a firm hold on the ball. Three more men. He had to put them out. Had to. It meant more than a victory—it meant a chance of keeping baseball at Tech for at least another year. Ted glanced at the bench. He saw his dad, square-jawed, anxious-eyed Tim Moran, gazing in his direction. Ted smiled tiredly and the veteran coach looked relieved. He grinned back and that was all Ted needed.

Ted quickly struck out the first two batters to face him. But the next man up was Rocky Stone. Rocky swaggered up to the plate. There was a confident smirk on his face.

Ted pitched his fast ball. He put everything into it. Rocky swung—and missed. The fans yelled noisily. Rocky Stone grimaced. This time he didn't look so confident. He stood there waiting again. And again it was Ted's fast ball that added the second strike. As Ted prepared to pitch again, Rocky Stone suddenly backed away from the plate. The umpire called for time out.

"I have a piece of dirt in my eye," Rocky complained, rubbing his eye. "I can't see a thing."

"Aw, you're just getting an alibi ready," Pudge grunted. "Get back up there and strike out like a gentleman."

Rocky Stone glared at the pudgy Tech catcher. He rubbed his eye a few more times and then stepped back up to the plate. Out on the pitcher's mound Ted had seen the whole affair. He wasn't letting himself be fooled. The dust wasn't blowing and there was no reason for Rocky to have anything in his eye. So Ted once again threw his fast ball.

The ball streaked for the plate. Rocky Stone lunged into it—and missed. The game was over and Tech had done the impossible.

The team was in the locker room dressing when Coach Moran came in. "Snap it up, fellows. In half an hour you have to be in the auditorium. This is Award Day, you know."

That was enough to hurry all of them. Soon they were in the midst of the award assembly. Various athletic and scholastic achievements were rewarded. Finally it came time to award the baseball letters. Coach Moran made a short speech.

"I have good news for the school," he said. "Because our boys defeated State today, it has been decided that Tech should again have a ball team next year. It hasn't been generally known—but until our victory, we weren't going to be able to have a team."

A roar of spontaneous applause rolled through the auditorium. The coach held up his hands. When there was silence, he said, "We have one more year to prove ourselves. As you know, our grandstand is small and we cannot accommodate large crowds. As a result our gate receipts have not been enough to make baseball profitable. If only we had a larger grandstand, we could take in more money. Then we wouldn't have to ask for outside help to finance our baseball program. I'm hoping that in some manner we'll be able to finance the grandstand before next season. But right now it doesn't look promising."

The awards were made and as Ted and Pudge walked back to their seats, Pudge said, "I wonder why they're keeping us here? All the awards have been given. We should be finished."

"I'm wondering the same thing myself," Ted commented.

But the two athletes did not have to wait long for their answer. The president of the school mounted the platform.

"And now," he said, "it comes time to make a special award. A great sportsman, a man whose generosity knows no bounds, has set up a fund that will provide a summer camp for outdoor-minded young men. Beginning this year this sportsman, Colonel Cassiday, will pay the expenses of two outstanding men from every college in this section to his camp. The camp is located in the heart of the Rockies. This year, after long and careful deliberation, the committee on awards has chosen two young men who typify the spirit of Tech. These men have made reputations for themselves in both the classroom and on the athletic field. Now at this time it is my honor and privilege to award these students a full summer at the All-American Camp with all expenses paid by Colonel Cassiday.

"If Ted Moran and Pudge Lawson will step up onto the platform, I will award them their entrance certificates. I also have two railroad tickets to the Rocky Mountain region. I'm sure the entire school joins me in extending good wishes to these fortunate young men."

Down in the student section, Ted Moran sat stupefied. He turned to Pudge. Pudge, too, was spellbound.

It was Ted who recovered first. He reached over, shook Pudge.

"He's calling for us," Ted whispered. "Let's get up there quick—before we wake up or he changes his mind." The pair got up, and amidst rounds of applause, walked up onto the stage. Ted Moran's heart was singing. Already he was thinking that next week he would be in the mountains, headed for high adventure. His dream, at last, had come true . . .

2. THE ALL-AMERICAN CAMP

"Ted. Ted Moran. Wake up."

Ted Moran opened his eyes sleepily. "Hey, wait a minute," he mumbled. "What's the idea of getting me out of bed in the middle of the night? Wha—oh, it's you, Pudge."

Pudge Lawson stood in the aisle of the swiftly moving streamlined train that was carrying them toward the green, forested slopes of the Rockies. Pudge was already dressed and he stood there holding the curtain aside, peering into Ted's berth.

"It isn't the middle of the night. It's morning. How you can sleep when you're headed for the swellest vacation in the world is more than I can see. Hurry and get dressed. I want you to come into the observation car with me and look out the windows. I've never seen such scenery."

"Personally," Ted said, "I got my fill of the plains yesterday. You get pretty tired of looking at country so

21

level that a ten-foot hump in the road looks like a mountain."

"That shows what you know about streamliners. While we were sleeping, this train was burning up miles. You've got a small window there in your berth. Pull the curtain back and take a look."

Ted Moran did just that—and got the surprise of his life.

"Wh—why we're in the mountains already. Sa-aay, we did make good time last night. Well, I'm not waiting any longer. These brown eyes of mine have never beheld the splendor of mountain scenery. I'm ready to take in the sights. Come on, Pudge. Shake it up. Well, what are you waiting for?"

"I'm waiting for you," Pudge grinned. "I think you'd feel more comfortable in the observation car if you took off your pajamas and put on your clothes."

Ted reddened. "If you ever tell on me, the gang back home will kid me for weeks!"

"How can you think of things back home? We're headed for adventure."

Ted hurried through dressing and this time, when he went into the observation car, it was to stay there. For the sights that unfolded before him as the train swept up the canyon were breath-taking.

Neither Ted nor Pudge had ever been in the mountains before. The sight of the Rockies, the largest, most ruggedly beautiful range of mountains in North America, was enough to keep them enthralled.

The railroad track twisted and turned up through the rugged canyons. On one side was a sheer cliff of rock that extended high into the air. On the other side the two young men could look below, down steep canyon drops to the winding sliver of ribbon that was the stream.

After gazing down at the view for some time Pudge said soberly, "Look, Ted, I've been asking everyone a lot of questions since I learned we were going to get to go to the All-American Camp. Everyone says that in summer camps you learn things about the woods, like tracking someone through the woods. Or how to find your way back to civilization when you're lost."

Ted said, "You can bet your boots I'm going to learn everything about these mountains that I can. I'd hate to be lost out there and not have an idea how to get back. Say, Pudge, wouldn't it be something if you and I got lost?"

"Huh?" Pudge frowned as he looked at Ted. "Us get lost? How could that happen? We won't have a chance to get lost if we stay with someone who knows his way around." Pudge shivered involuntarily. "Why do you have to talk of such things? Now I suppose I'll be dreaming of mountain lions jumping out from behind rocks to nab me. Say, do you suppose there are really mountain lions up here in these mountains?"

"Search me," Ted said. "Personally, I don't see how any kind of an animal could live up here. There doesn't seem to be much to eat that I can see. . . ."

Half an hour later the streamliner slid to a noiseless halt beside a small mountain station. Ted and Pudge hustled from the train along with a dozen other young men. Armed with bulging suitcases, they stood there on the platform along with the others. The train pulled out and for a moment they were alone. The railroad station attendant came out onto the platform.

"You boys headed for the All-American Camp? I thought so. Your bus will be here in a minute. Ah, here it comes now. Indian Jim is driving."

A long yellow bus pulled up over a rise in the road, halted beside the platform. A tall, lordly red man jumped out from behind the wheel. He was clad in buckskin clothes, heavily ornamented with bright, shiny beads. He wore moccasins and as he moved over the platform, one had to look at him to realize that he was there, for he moved without making a sound. He stopped in front of the boys.

"Welcome," he said. "Me Indian Jim."

The two Tech athletes climbed into the bus with the rest. Ted, who was seated directly behind the driver, leaned forward and said, "When do we get to camp, Indian Jim?"

"Not until morning. First we cross high mountain covered with snow. Then we go down other side to green valley beside big lake."

Ted leaned back. Upon his face was a look of anticipation and contentment. He had seen the high, snow-capped peaks around him and now he was going to get a chance to cross that snow. It was the first week in June and Ted was beginning to feel the sting of the cold mountain air. He sat there enjoying the sights throughout the rest of the day. At dusk the bus reached a high point in the narrow road and stopped. There was a small building off to the side of the road.

"All out," Indian Jim said. "Go no farther."

Wonderingly, Ted and Pudge followed the others inside. There they were met by a tall, well-built young man of about twenty-five. He was wearing a form-fitting uniform of a military green. His face was bronzed, almost as dark as that of Indian Jim.

"You fellows are probably starved," he smiled. "Take off your coats and you'll find a nice hot meal waiting." The entire group skinned out of coats and hats and as they were taking their places at the table, the uniformed man continued.

"I'm not connected with the All-American Camp. I am a forest ranger. Part of my job is to see that every visitor in these parts has a good time. I'm here to help you. Right now while you're eating, I want to pass

along a few words of advice. First, you've probably noticed that you have more difficulty breathing, more at
least than you did at your homes. The reason is the
high altitude. Up here at an elevation of nine thousand
feet above sea level, the air is rarified. It seems to take
more air to breathe than it does down lower. But don't
let that bother you. In a day or two your bodies will
readjust themselves to the surroundings and you'll
never know that anything has happened.

"You'll learn that you have to dress for the weather.
Tonight we're going to have a long ride and it will be
a cold one. Get into your heaviest clothing. I don't
want anyone to be uncomfortable. There's one surprise that I've saved until last. Instead of going the rest
of the way by bus, we go by horse-drawn sled. The road,
the rest of the way, is covered with snow."

It was Ted who said, "How can we go by sled when
there isn't any snow around here? There's snow on the
peaks up above us—but we didn't see any as we came up
here."

The ranger smiled. "Well, that's a fair question.
But I'll wait and let you see the answer for yourselves.
Get dressed now. It's time we were leaving. Indian Jim
and I have to be back here for the next bunch of boys
who will arrive tomorrow."

Ten minutes later, wearing heavy wool clothing,
topped by a heavy mackinaw jacket, Ted followed their

leaders. They walked up a short, granite-covered road. The ranger was talking. "You will observe that you came up here on the south side of the mountain. Now we've reached the top. Well here we are. You see, on this north side there is snow. In the mountains the snow sometimes remains on the north slopes throughout the summer. You see, the sun doesn't hit it there."

There was a long, boxlike affair with runners under it instead of wheels. A team of white horses stood hitched in readiness. "There are seats for all," the ranger told them. "Climb in and bundle up."

Thus began the final leg of the journey to the All-American Camp. There was something pleasant about the way the sleigh slid along through the piled drifts. The horses were wearing collars with bells and there was a merry, peaceful jingle that made sleep inviting. Curled up in a blanket, Ted Moran thought it would be easy to sleep, but his mind would not allow him to sleep at all. There were so many things he wanted to know. What kind of high adventure awaited him at the end of this ride? He saw that the forest ranger was awake. Ted moved over beside him.

"I have a hundred questions," Ted said. "Would it make you angry if I asked you to answer some of them for me?"

The ranger's grin was visible in the moonlight. "Not at all. What is it?"

"This All-American Camp," Ted asked. "What about it? What do they do there? What is the purpose of it?"

"The purpose is quite simple. Colonel Cassiday has a lot of money. Because he likes young men, because he is so fond of outdoor living himself, he has established this camp so that young college fellows like yourself can learn more about nature. As for the camp—I've never seen a finer one."

"What will we do to spend our time? Play baseball, or have track meets, or what?" Ted asked.

"Oh, there won't be much time for baseball. You're in the mountains now. You'll learn woodcraft and how to fish and hunt and trap. There's the gate of the camp up ahead. See it?"

As the sled slowed down, Ted, in his eagerness, jumped over the side.

Too late Ted saw a man loom up almost before his eyes. He tried to catch himself but it was too late. He had knocked the figure down and had, himself, landed in a snowdrift. He righted himself swiftly, an apology already forming on his lips. But the apology froze there. For the man he had hit was none other than Rocky Stone of State College.

"Oh, so it's you," Rocky sneered. Then a smile of anticipation crossed his dark face. "It's Ted Moran, the big athlete from the little hick college. Well, I'm glad to see you here. We're meeting again sooner than I had hoped."

Ted didn't like the sound of Rocky's voice. But he wasn't giving ground. He squared his shoulders, thrust his strong young chin forward. "Yes," he said evenly, "we do meet again. And I feel the same as you, Rocky. I'm not a bit sorry."

3. A DAY IN CAMP

THE camp was far nicer than Ted had dreamed. In the center of a clearing was a large building. This Ted guessed to be the mess hall as well as a meeting place. At the edge of the clearing, shaped in a circle, were at least thirty cabins. And what cabins they were!

Their exteriors were of native logs and they looked like the cabins of pioneers. Beside each cabin was a stone fireplace for outside cooking. Stretching back of the cabins were dozens of mountain peaks, looking in the early morning sun like great, giant-sized ice-cream cones. They were covered with snow and timber.

The other campers piled out of the sleigh. Pudge rubbed his eyes sleepily. Pudge and Ted started to walk toward the large administration hall in the center of the camp where the forest ranger told them to report. Ted lowered his voice. "Do you know who I bumped into on this end? Rocky Stone is enrolled here for the summer."

Pudge pulled up short. His mouth fell open. "That guy?" he said in swift surprise. "Boy, what a pleasant summer this is going to be. I'll spend so much time keeping you two from each other's throats that I won't have time to hunt and fish."

The words were half in jest, but behind them was a quiet seriousness that Ted did not miss. He said, "I feel the same as you do, Pudge. I think Rocky Stone is a trouble maker and he's out to make it as annoying for me as possible. One thing is certain, though, I'm not going to encourage him. But neither am I going to run from him. If he wants to be disagreeable, I think I can take care of myself."

They had reached the main building now. They walked up the wide stone steps, across the veranda and into a large waiting room. Twenty or thirty fellows were sitting around, looking at books and magazines. Pudge and Ted eased into chairs, began to look about them. What they saw was a large, comfortable room whose walls were covered with stuffed hunting trophies. There were deer, moose, bear and elk heads in profusion. The walls were also covered with large, sleek-looking mounted fish.

Time passed swiftly and almost before they realized it, the sun was well up in the sky and they were beginning to feel warm under the heavy clothing. A man walked out of a small office on the north end of the room. He stepped up onto a platform.

"I'd like to have your attention for a minute, fellows."

While the room was growing silent, Ted studied the man. He looked to be around forty years of age. He was not a large man, but he had a well-groomed, impressive look about him. He was of medium height and his temples were beginning to turn gray. His face was tanned and his eyes were wrinkled from staring at the sun. When he spoke, he had a soft but commanding voice.

"I'm Jeff Jones," the man announced, "the camp director. At this time I'm not going to outline your program for the summer for all the campers aren't here. However, I will say this much—I'm glad you're here and I'm promising you that you're going to spend the most exciting summer of your lives. You'll fish and hunt and trap. You'll live in the woods just as the Indians and pioneers used to live. But to save time, I'm going to wait until the rest of the campers arrive tomorrow, before calling our first camp meeting.

"You'll find your cabin number on the list on the bulletin board. I would suggest that you go there now. Change your clothes. From then on you can do as you please. Today there will be no regular lunch or supper periods—all you will have to do is come to the dining hall when you're hungry.

"There are boats at the lake. If you go boating, be careful. Perhaps some of you will even want to fish.

Each boy has a fishing rod and trout flies as well as a line. You'll find this equipment waiting in your cabin. Well, that's all, fellows. You're on your own until tomorrow morning."

Ten minutes later Ted and Pudge were unpacking. Their cabin was large enough to house eight fellows. There were four sets of wall bunks and Ted and Pudge chose a set near the windows that overlooked the large lake.

Ted stood there in the window, gazing below. "The lake must be at least a mile long. Boy, what fish there must be in it. I believe there are other lakes . . . why, of course. Look up ahead there, Pudge. This lake runs into a small stream and the stream connects with another lake. I can't wait to get down there."

"Me, too—but how about fishing? We have these fishing outfits. I don't know anything about them—but I'm willing to learn. I guess each of us gets a pole. There's one fishing kit under each set of bunks so I suppose we're to share it. Here, open it—let's see what's inside."

Ted unlocked the square green tin box. The box contained several spools of line, a box of queer-looking trout flies and several other fishing accessories.

"We've got time to look at it after we get down to breakfast," Ted exclaimed. "Come on—I'm starving."

Breakfast over, they hurried outside. Ted carried the box and Pudge carried two hollow tubes that contained the jointed poles. A path led down toward the lake through tall fir trees, and rocky boulders. Rounding a turn, Ted pulled up short.

"Hey, look what I see." Ted pointed toward a small clearing. "It's Indian Jim. Indian Jim! I want to see you a minute."

It was indeed the Indian who had brought them to the camp. As Ted and Pudge approached, he looked up, grinned.

"I thought you were going back to get some more fellows," Ted said. "What are you doing there?"

"Indian Jim decide stay here. He send other man back. Indian Jim like to practice before tenderfeet arrive."

"Look, Indian Jim," Ted said. "If you want to practice something, how would you like to practice fishing? Pudge and I are tenderfeet as you say. We don't know a thing about the sport."

Indian Jim grinned. "Indian Jim like fish plenty."

The trio went down to the lake together. There they found several boats tied to a dock. Indian Jim stepped into the largest boat on silent, moccasined feet. He motioned the two young men to follow him. When they were seated, Jim took the two oars in hand, then rowing in a faultless, easy motion, pulled out into the lake.

"Tenderfeet look down. See many strange things."

Ted looked overside. Below was water as clear as drinking water. The bottom of the lake was clearly visible. It consisted of millions of rocky pebbles. The sun was glistening on them, sending up a kind of showery brilliance.

"Can you beat that," Ted exclaimed. "At home the creek that runs through the edge of town is so muddy that you couldn't see six inches below the surface. And here it must be at least three feet to the bottom."

"Ho, ho," the red man laughed. "Tenderfeet think water only yard deep. Very funny. Look, Indian Jim show tenderfeet how funny his talk is."

Indian Jim reached for the hollow tube that contained the fishing pole Ted had brought for himself. The pole was in three sections. It was made of bamboo and each section was smaller around than the other. Indian Jim jointed the sections together and had a regulation length trout pole ten feet long. Each section of the pole contained small eyelets through which the line was to be threaded. But before threading the line, Indian Jim took the pole by the small end, dropped it over the side. To Ted's surprise, the pole touched the bottom and only a few inches of the tip was out of the water.

"Never trust eye in mountain water. Look shallow, but sometimes very deep," Indian Jim said. "Clear water play many tricks, even on oldtimer like Indian Jim. Now, Jim show tenderfeet how to put lines together."

The friendly man opened Ted's kit and took out one

of the spools of line. Then he took a metal spool with a small handle on it which clamped to the pole's handle and worked like a windlass. Jim explained that the metal spool was called a reel and that it was to wind in the line when a fish was hooked. He took the line from the wooden spool, wound it onto the metal reel. Then threading the line down through the eyelets on the pole, he handed it to Ted.

"Next take fly and tie to end of line. If trout like fly, he take it quick. Some days trout don't like anything."

Ted began to look over his selection of flies. Each fly, he discovered, was made up of many small, multi-colored feathers. Each fly contained a small, sharp-pointed hook. The hook was well-hidden by the feathers.

"Mountain trout very smart," Indian Jim said. "He not eat fly that don't look right. Each fly looks like some kind of bug or fly—trout come along, bite into fly, and bingo! he get stuck with hook. Tenderfeet reel trout in fast or he tear up line and get away. Understand?"

Ted grinned. "Yes, I understand. Look, here's a fly that looks like a bee. Here's another that is a dead ringer for a dragonfly. Here's a black gnat. Say, this is going to be fun. All I have to do is throw the line out into the water and wait for the fish to bite, huh?"

"That's all," Indian Jim said. "But not easy. You see."

Ted unreeled about ten feet of line. Then lifting the pole high overhead, he whipped it around, trying to throw the line out in front of him. But the slender, limber pole was unwieldy. It threw the line out crookedly. The hook, or fly, sailed past Jim's ear. The Indian fell flat in the bottom of the boat.

He grunted, "Paleface say Indian scalpum plenty. Indian say tenderfeet with sharp fishhook scalp anyone who standing close by. Look, let Jim show you how to cast trout fly."

Indian Jim took the pole from the embarrassed Ted. He reeled out about thirty feet of line. Then Jim brought the pole straight up over his shoulder. The limber pole snapped back and the snap jerked the entire length of line out behind him. Then in a swift motion that bent the pole in an arc, Indian Jim brought the pole straight down until it was level with his shoulder and extending straight out in front of him. The line shot out and fell flat upon the water ahead. The artificial fly lay on the top of the water, looking as natural as if it were real. Slowly Jim began to drag the line in by turning the handle on his reel. The fly had moved about ten feet when suddenly things began to happen.

First there was a streak of silver through the water. It travelled like a surface torpedo. Next the pole seemed to bend double. The line stretched out taut. There was a churn of silver spray where the fly had been but an instant before. Then a fish leaped high out of the water. It wasn't a large fish—only about a foot long. But to Ted and Pudge it looked to be at least as large as a small shark. The fish was a beautiful specimen. Its sides were sparkling and as the sun fell upon the leaping fish, every color seemed to come out, making it look like something an artist had just painted.

"Boy, what a beauty," Ted exclaimed. "That thing looks exactly like a rainbow." The trout arched its back, then plunged straight down again. Indian Jim was letting the line run out again. The fish was hooked and was going away from the boat.

"Fish look like rainbow," Jim said quietly. "Maybe that's why fish is called rainbow trout. Watch Jim. If I pull fish in now, he fight line and maybe break it. So I let him go. When he get tired, I pull him in and have fish tonight. Understand?"

"Sure," Ted said. "You keep all the slack out of the line. Because if you didn't, the fish might jerk the line and break it loose. That's logical enough."

After playing the fish for about three minutes, Jim began to reel it in. Soon the trout was up beside the boat. Pudge, who had been too interested to move, now said, "Lift him over the side of the boat, Jim."

The red man grunted. "Mister rainbow not too tired yet. When fisherman lift a trout into air, fisherman go home without trout. Watch." The Indian lifted the trout out of the water. Instantly the fish began to thresh about and had not the red man immediately dropped the line into the water, the fish would have broken loose. "Lifting trout no good. Watch Jim. See, reach into water. Run thumb along line until you come to fish's mouth. Put thumb in mouth and finger in gill. Hold tight. That way trout never get away."

And just as easy as that, the Indian brought the fish over the side. Pudge reached for the rainbow. "Let me hold him," Pudge exclaimed. But Jim motioned toward the water.

"Wet hands. Good sportsman always handle fish with wet hands. That way fish not get hurt. See, like this."

Indian Jim wet his left hand and then removed the trout from the hook. Next he thrust another line through the trout's mouth and then, tying one end to the boat, threw the trout back into the water. Jim handed the line back to Ted.

"Now you try," he said. "Maybe you catch big fish."

Ted took the line. Eagerly, he tried to duplicate Jim's motions. At first it was awkward. But gradually he smoothed out his cast so that he could lay the length of line out almost exactly as he wanted it. The fly that had hooked the fish for Indian Jim simply wouldn't lure another. So Ted decided to change. He looked through his box until he found a large blue dragonfly with a hook carefully concealed in the body. This he attached to the line.

"Row over around those rocks along the shore." Ted

said. "I've heard that trout sometimes hide under rocks."

Jim smiled appreciatively. "Tenderfeet use head. Rocks are dark. Big trout hide in shadows to eat little trout that swim by."

Ted waited until they were about twenty feet from shore. Then he flipped the dragonfly toward a rock. The fly fell on the water, about an ich from a large, partly submerged rock. For an instant the dragonfly sat there bobbing up and down on the small ripples. What happened next neither Ted nor Pudge nor Indian Jim could be sure. Afterward they could not agree on it. But Ted's idea was this:

There was a bath of flying spray. It was as if half a dozen motorboats had been turned loose and were churning up the water. Next a fish leaped high out of the water. Not just a small fish, but a huge, glimmering fellow that almost frightened Ted. The fish arched its beautiful back in the sun, turned over so that its white, smooth belly cast off the sun's brilliant rays. Then it plunged to the depths. Furiously Ted began to reel in. But it was no use. His line had snapped as cleanly as if he had hooked into a freight train.

"Oh—can you beat that," Ted said disappointedly. "I had a chance to catch him and I missed him. I feel terrible."

Jim's face was suddenly very solemn.

"Tenderfeet no need to feel bad. Tenderfeet should

feel good indeed. That fish been here for years. He the old granddaddy of all the trout in the lake. For years many fishermen come here to try to catch Brown Beauty. Many fishermen hook him, but Brown Beauty not get caught. He a smart, sly old fish. He no fool."

Ted sat back amazed. His blood was already pounding madly through his veins. So this was what was in store for him at the camp! His heart ached to get another chance at the legendary Brown Beauty—yet even though he was not a fisherman, his instinct told him that it would be a long time before the beautiful old fish was fooled again. Ted knew that he had been lucky even hooking into the scarred old fighter. But as he slowly tied on another line, he said, half to himself, "Brown Beauty old fellow, from now on you and I are going to duel each other at every opportunity. I'll never forget the way you surprised me today. The next time I'm going to do my best to surprise you . . ."

Little did Ted realize how much work he would have to go to before that promise was to come true.

4. SADDLE AND RIDE

"Gentlemen, I'm happy to stand here and welcome you to this first meeting of the All-American Camp." Jeff Jones, the camp director, stood on the platform in the lounge of the administration building. It was the second morning Ted and Pudge had been in camp. Now all of the campers had arrived. Pudge and his athletic companion were seated in the front row, listening.

"This morning," the camp director continued, "I'm going to take a bit of your time, telling you what to expect here. Then after it's all done, I promise you that you'll be in for a thrill. Tonight we're all going to sleep out in the open, miles from any human habitation."

There was an enthusiastic burst of applause. Ted turned to Pudge, nudged him. "Nothing slow about them around here," he commented. "They start doing things with a bang."

Jeff Jones held up his hands for silence. "The first thing I must tell you young men is this: here in the Rockies, the old law of nature is very evident. That law

43

is the survival of the fittest. It applies to animals and it applies to humans. Here every day you are away from camp, you will be pitting yourselves against strong outside forces. There will be the ever-present danger of swift mountain storms. They descend almost without a moment's notice. Sometimes they're over swiftly. At other times they're apt to last for several days. Unless you know how to take care of yourselves, you will find the going exceedingly difficult. But storms are only minor irritations. There is little human habitation here. Because of this fact, there is an abundance of wild life. And I might make it clear once and for all—wild animals are dangerous under certain, given conditions. This is particularly so of the mountain lion, the wolf and the grizzly bear.

"But more of all this later, fellows. It is not my purpose to try to frighten you. Rather, it is the aim of this camp to teach young men how to cope with nature's powerful forces. When you leave here, each of you should be able to live in the woods without artificial aid. You should know how to protect yourselves against the elements as well as the animals. You should be able to hunt and fish with the most primitive weapons.

"A long time ago Colonel Cassiday got the idea of doing something for worthy boys of college age and finally he hit upon the idea of this camp. This is the first season and while there may be a few wrinkles to be ironed out, I'm sure you will learn that the whole idea has been very well planned.

"Your life here will be regulated to schedule. Every morning you must be up at six and have breakfast by seven. After the morning chores are taken care of, you will be more or less on your own, to do as you see fit—except, of course, when we have group hikes or contests. Your life here will be a pleasant one. Instead of telling you not to do things, it will be our job to tell you things you can do. Of course, there are certain things that, for the good of the entire camp, you must refrain from doing. I'll mention them briefly:

"First, don't go near the water unless you are with someone who can swim. Second, don't stray from the camp after ten o'clock. I'm not trying to tell you that it is too dangerous—for in most cases it wouldn't be. But at night it is very easy to become lost in the mountains—and there is always the chance that a hungry bear might wander down in search of a bite of fresh meat. So, for these reasons, the ten o'clock rule will be strictly enforced. Any camper who is caught violating it will be punished by having some of his privileges cancelled.

"I'm not going to keep you much longer this morning. However, I'm sure that each of you has some kind of question. I'll answer them as quickly as possible. Who is first?"

Ted Moran had been puzzled by one thing. Now he

said, "You spoke of contests. Did you mean sports, or what?"

The camp director smiled. "I'm glad you brought that question up. I was leaving out an important part of my speech. Yes, there will be contests. I imagine they will be hard fought. In fact, Colonel Cassiday wants them to be—and for that reason we are awarding a small gold star to the camper who proves himself to be the best all-round competitor. The gold star will be awarded by Colonel Cassiday himself—and the camper who earns it will be known as the Gold Star Camper."

"How do you get the award?" the question was asked by Rocky Stone, and as he voiced it, his eyes were fastened upon Ted Moran. It was evident that Rocky was already planning to win the award himself.

"We have devised a point award system," the camp director said. "For various competitions, points will be awarded. I have posted a list of the points upon the bulletin board. For example, the camper who proves to be the best in hunting will be awarded one hundred points. Second best will get fifty—and so on.

"Now there's one more part of the contest. There are more than two hundred fellows in camp. With so many young men living together, there will be accidents, close calls—in fact, almost anything can happen, and probably will. Certain situations will call for quick thinking and exemplary leadership. To the camper who, in the opinion of myself and Colonel Cassiday,

performs the best deed of the camp period, a special
bonus of one hundred and fifty points will be awarded.
Now is there anything else?"

"Yes," one camper asked. "When do we get to meet
Colonel Cassiday? When do we get to thank him?"

"You must all realize," Jeff Jones answered, "that
Colonel Cassiday is a very busy man. However, before
the camp period is over, Colonel Cassiday will be here
to see how well his plan is working. And as I have already said—the Colonel will personally award the gold
star to the best camper. Well, I believe we have taken
up enough of your time this morning. For half an hour
you may do whatever you wish. But remember, when
your time is up, be back here and be sure to have your
overnight outfits with you."

The meeting broke up immediately. As for Ted and
Pudge, the two just sat there in the front row, staring
at each other. There was a faraway look in Ted's eyes.
"You know," he said softly, "nothing would please me
more than to win that gold star. But it wouldn't be
the trophy I was so interested in, Pudge. Most medals
are just something to stick away in a drawer and forget in a few years. But this would be different. Because
to get it, a fellow would have to know plenty about
these mountains. That was what I was thinking of
when Jeff Jones made the announcement."

They went to the bulletin board and along with
many other young campers, stood there, eagerly scan-

ning the list of point awards. What they saw was this:

POINT AWARD LIST

Event	1st	2nd	3rd
Trapping	100	50	25
Hunting (wolves)	100	50	25
Woodcraft	100	50	25
Fishing (largest trout)	100	50	25
Swimming (high point man)	50	30	10
Track (high point man)	50	30	10
Baseball (best all-around man)	50	30	10
Best deed of camp period	150	..	..

Note: This is primarily a summer camp and for this reason, special attention will be given to Trapping, Hunting, Woodcraft and Fishing. Regular athletic events, while important to keep campers in good physical trim, will take up only a small part of your time and for this reason, fewer points will be awarded to men proficient in them.

In addition to this gold star to the best all-round camper, the school from which the camper comes will also be given a magnificent award by Colonel Cassiday. This gift, in the form of money, will be used by the school to further athletic activity.

Ted had been reading the point award list with only casual interest. But when his eyes came to the last paragraph, there was an immediate quickening of interest.

"Pudge. Come on." Ted's voice was low, but when he spoke that way, Pudge knew it was time to act.

Pudge fell in beside him. Ted walked across the lounge, knocked at the door of the camp director's office. He heard the call to come in.

"Pardon me for intruding," Ted said, as they stepped inside. "But there is one thing that isn't quite clear to me. I notice there will be a special award to the school from which the Gold Star Camper comes. Would you mind explaining that a bit?"

Jeff Jones looked immediately interested. "So the idea has already appealed to someone," he said, his eyes twinkling. "I'm glad to hear it. Well suppose we use you as an example. Your school chose you to come to this camp because it believed you to be outdoors-minded, athletically inclined and eager to learn more about nature.

"Now, suppose you prove to be the best man in camp. Your school's judgment is upheld. The school has the honor of having turned out a perfect example of American manhood. For that reason Colonel Cassiday has decided that the school should receive a reward that will enable it to turn out more young men of such a type. The reward, as the bulletin states, will be in the form of money. The school is to use the money in the athletic program so that more boys will be able to participate in sports. Now do you understand?"

"Yes . . . but, how much money? A thousand dollars?"

The camp director smiled indulgently. "Oh, see here, now," he exclaimed. "You seem to forget that Colonel Cassiday is a very generous man. What could a college do with a thousand dollars? Colonel Cassiday's check will be for the sum of fifty thousand dollars."

"Fifty thousand dollars!" The sum was beyond the scope of his wildest dreams. For a moment he stood there, unable to say a word. But the news had had a strange effect upon him.

"And that money is to be used as the school's athletic department sees fit? To build a grandstand, for instance?" he asked.

"Of course," the camp director smiled. "If the school needs a grandstand, I'm sure it would be a splendid way to use the money. And—why are you leaving so soon?"

"I've got to get outside where I can shout," Ted laughed.

And a moment later Ted and his roly-poly companion were outside. The sun had come out warm and the snow on the ground was melting. Before many more hours the only snow left would be on the peaks and the north slopes.

"Do you understand what this means?" Ted exclaimed as they walked toward their cabin. "It means that Tech has a chance to get that grandstand after all.

Just think what we could do with that money. We would build a grandstand first. Then with teams from larger colleges coming to play us, we would draw big crowds. Baseball would pay large dividends and we could have a team every season without having to ask the athletic governing board for money. It would assure Dad of his coaching job."

"Yeah," Pudge exclaimed. "Yeah, it would be wonderful. But don't forget one thing—you have to win that award. I don't have to remind you that there are a lot of fellows in this camp who probably have the same idea as you. Particularly a guy named Rocky Stone."

Ted sobered. "Look, Pudge, until a few minutes ago this point award business was just something to make the summer pass pleasantly. But now it's the most serious thing that ever happened. I'm going after it."

"Well," Pudge said slowly, "when you go after a thing, you usually don't stop until you either get it, or push someone else into it."

They reached their cabin, went inside. Each set of bunks had a large drawer underneath. Ted opened the drawer. He found two large packages, each labeled: OVERNIGHT OUTFIT. Ted tossed one of the packages to Pudge. The other he unwrapped. What he found was a roll of woolen blankets. Unrolling them, he found other articles. There was a small flashlight, an oilskin package containing matches, a small hatchet, a hunting knife, and a thin, waterproof sheet.

"This thing," Ted said, examining the sheet, "has me puzzled. What do you suppose it is?"

"Search me," Pudge said. "We'll have to wait and find out."

Ted rolled his things back up into a tight, compact bundle. This he strapped into a roll, then hung it over his shoulders. He found that it was quite easy to carry that way. Next he picked up his tube that contained the fishing pole. Pudge brought the tackle box and, taking his own bed roll, followed Ted toward the Administration Building. There they found the rest of the campers.

"Fellows," Jeff Jones said, "this is to be your first overnight trip. Indian Jim is down at the stable. The horses are all ready to be saddled. We're leaving at once."

"Horses!" the exclamation was general. Nothing had been said about horses.

The stable was down the hill to the south, completely out of view from the camp. It was a large, rambling barn and it was built in a circle so that the center formed a corral. It was in that center clearing that the campers found Indian Jim. He surveyed his charges.

"Tenderfeet saddle own horses. Horses gentle like little billy goats. Watch Jim first."

Indian Jim went into the barn and came out leading a shiny black horse. A saddle was already lying
upon the ground. Jim took a small blanket, put it on
the horse's back. Then he lifted the saddle up also.
There was a band that was much like a belt hanging
from the saddle. Jim pulled the belt tight around the
horse's body to keep the saddle from slipping.

As the red man worked, Jeff Jones explained, "You
will all be expected to saddle your own horses as Jim
has told you. So pay attention to how it is done. The
saddle blanket is to keep the saddle from rubbing the
horse's back. The strap that holds the saddle in place
is called the cinch. You will observe that Jim is now
putting the bridle on the horse. That piece of iron is
called the bit. See how he is placing it in the horse's
mouth—and those two long straps—they are reins and
are used to control the horse. That's all there is to it.
Each set of boys will find horses in the stalls that corre-
spond to your cabin and bunk numbers. Go ahead.
Get your horses and bring them out here."

In a moment Ted and his heavy companion were
staring at a stall that contained a beautiful red and
white spotted mount—a pinto pony. Pudge said, "Boy,
what a beauty."

"See," Ted exclaimed, "old Spot likes us already.
Look at him nuzzle that nose at you. Go ahead, rub
his nose for him."

Pudge did just that and the horse shook his mane

contentedly. "I can see right now," Ted said, "where there's something to this cowboy business. Well, let's get outside. Spot seems as anxious to go as I do."

They took Spot outside and Pudge followed with the shiny leather saddle. They took but a few moments to saddle the horse. Ted let Pudge climb up first—then he put his foot in the stirrup and got on behind. Pudge took the reins and gave the left one a slight jerk. Spot turned to the left and began to walk through the corral gate and out into the open. Other horses were already out there.

They waited awhile until all the others were ready. Then Indian Jim rode out. "Jim go first. Tenderfeet follow. Trail up mountain steep in places. Tenderfeet go slow."

Thus began the ride. For an hour the caravan alternated between a walk and a slow trot. From the front of the caravan, Jeff Jones said, "We're eating lunch at that place on the flat rocks up ahead."

5. UNWELCOME VISITOR

THEY rode onto the flat ledge of rock. The order was given to dismount. Each rider found a handy tree where the horses were tied. The flat rock was really nothing but the top of a bare boulder. It was quite large, covering an area of about one hundred square feet. There was plenty of room for a campfire. The rock overlooked a canyon and the boys could see a small, gurgling stream a few yards below.

On the other side of the rock was a steep slope that went upward. The slope was covered with thousands of shapely, fragrant-smelling pines.

"You can all unsaddle," Jeff Jones said. "While you're doing that, I'll tell you a few things to remember. When you are on a trip that requires horses, remember that the horse is just as important as the rider —for the horse is doing the most work. After each leg of the journey, the horse should be unsaddled and tied near water and feed. Down below you will find plenty

of grass along the bank of the stream. Your horses will
be quite content there."

The horses were taken below and when the campers
returned, the camp director had more to say to them.
"It is time to eat. But before doing that, we're going
to make camp—for this is where we intend to stay tonight. We're sheltered here and if a storm should come,
we would have this wall of rock to shelter us. Since
making camp requires a knowledge of woodcraft, I'm
going to let Indian Jim carry on from here."

The silent-walking redskin picked up his hatchet,
motioned for the others to follow. He walked—not
toward the stream—but away from it. The group followed the Indian off the ledge of rock and into the
timber. Soon they were on a gentle, tree-covered slope.
Indian Jim stopped beside a small tree. In fact, there
were two trees right together.

Jeff Jones explained, "A tree is one of the most valuable things in the mountains. Without the forests, the
mountains would be nothing more than dry-looking
piles of rock. A tree has a right to live and every camper
should protect the trees. That may sound queer when
I tell you that it is necessary to cut a tree to make your
shelter. But that can be explained.

"You will observe that Jim has stopped beside two
small trees. Each tree is about ten feet in height. But
notice. They are growing less than six inches apart.

Before long they will be crowding each other. Neither tree will be able to survive. So Jim is killing one of them. You will also notice that one of the trees has a place peeled off the bark. Every year the deer rub their antlers upon trees—and that is what has happened here. One tree has been injured—while the other is still quite healthy. So Jim is cutting the injured one. Remember that. A good woodsman never cuts down a tree that will grow into a fine specimen."

Indian Jim made a mark on the tree trunk—about three feet off the ground. Then swinging the hatchet four or five times, he cut a V-shaped nick about three fourths of the way through the trunk. When the tree began to lean over, Jim got a grip up high and pulled it down until the top tip was touching the ground. Quickly he cut the branches off close to the main trunk and in less than five minutes, he had the job finished. The base of the trunk extended up from the ground at right angles for about three feet. Then the tree sloped back down toward the ground. Jim took the waterproof sheet from his own bed roll. He said, "Indian Jim made tent quick."

Ted was beginning to understand. But he was still puzzled. He wondered how they could sleep there in comfort, particularly when there was still snow on the ground. But before he could ask the question, Jeff Jones said, "You will notice the snow on the ground.

That shouldn't bother a good camper. Up here it has not thawed yet. The snow is only a few inches deep. Underneath it is dry and warm. Watch."

The camp director, using his boot, kicked some of the snow aside. At once the ground became visible. It was generously covered with soft pine cones and brown needles that had fallen from the trees the year before. The surprising thing was that the needles were quite dry and when you stepped upon them, they were soft and springy.

"Pine cones," Indian Jim said, "make woodsman good mattress."

Jim got the snow out from beneath the tree he had cut. Then he spread his blankets out, making a fine bed. It took but a moment to stretch the waterproof sheet over the tree. By weighting the edges of the sheet with rocks, a small, cozy tent was formed. "If tender-feet no have tent," Jim explained, "green branches do almost as good."

Pudge and Ted fell to work making a tent for themselves. When their tent was pitched, both boys returned to the clearing where Indian Jim was busy making a fire. Several boys set to work carrying up old dead logs for firewood. The others sat around waiting.

Ted and Pudge walked to the edge of the cliff. "I wonder," Ted mused, "how the fishing would be down there?"

"You can't forget the way you tied into that trout yesterday, can you?" Pudge grinned.

"As a matter of fact, I can't," Ted admitted. "For one, I think I'll spend the afternoon trying to land myself some trout."

"Sounds like an excellent idea to me." Both boys turned. The speaker was the camp director. The gray-templed Jeff Jones said, "You'll find mountain stream fishing a great deal like lake fishing—except that you have to stay back out of sight. When a trout sees you, he's gone in a flash. If you get enough trout, you can roast them over an open fire and eat them for supper. How does that sound to you?"

"I can taste them already," Ted grinned.

Ted Moran was not speaking idly. Fishing appealed to him greatly. He had hardly tasted their lunch, although it was a good one. An entire side of fresh beef had been brought on a pack horse and the meal consisted of fried steak sandwiches, milk and potato salad. The provisions were kept in metal containers and after the meal, the containers were carried down and placed in the shallow icy stream so the food would not spoil.

Ted and Pudge rigged up their poles and cut down the valley toward the stream. They came upon it and Ted, stepping silently, peered out from behind a rock. He made a motion for Pudge to follow. Pudge looked to where Ted was pointing.

"Trout," Pudge whispered. "Look at them. Some of them are at least sixteen inches long. Well, what are we waiting for?"

Ted reached out with his line. But the shadow of his pole fell across the water. Instantly there were dozens of streaks of silver through the water. And then not a single trout was visible.

"Talk about greased lightning," Ted exclaimed, "that was sure it. That proves one thing, though. What we've heard about trout in streams is true. They won't be easy to catch."

The banks were well-covered by rocks and trees. Throwing out a line was going to be difficult. Ted said, "There won't be room for two of us. Suppose we split up. You go one direction and I'll go the other. We'll meet back here about the time the sun starts down beyond the range to the west of us. How about it?"

"Okay by me," Pudge said. "And the one who gets the fewest fish has to clean them. Is it a deal?"

"You've made a bargain."

Ted started up stream. He kept back away from the bank. At first he had difficulty casting. But gradually it became more natural. The flies were landing in the bubbling water, were being swept back down the stream just as a regular fly would be swept along if it happened to come too close to the water.

For half an hour nothing happened. Ted kept changing the color of his fly. He was using a bright red one from which trailed a shiny yellow feather. Ahead, and just around the bend, Ted saw a wall of rock. The water was dark near the rock ledge and was churning swiftly all around it. Ted remembered something Indian Jim had said about fish lying close to ledges in wait for something to eat. He had been fishing for quite a while without luck, so he decided to try his hunch.

Carefully he measured the distance. Then in an easy, whiplike motion, Ted brought his pole forward. The line shot out from the reel. The fly alighted in the water just a few feet above the dark, swirling eddy. It began to float down. Now it was only inches away. Now it was floating over the dark spot in the water. It was brushing up against the cliff. It was going to go past—

And then it happened! The fly disappeared in a swirl of white, churned-up foam. A dazzlingly marked brook trout leaped high out of the water, twisted and flipped in the air, trying to throw the hook from his mouth. But Ted was remembering the things he had been told. He reeled in rapidly until the line was taut. The fish fell back into the water and was off upstream. The line jerked out tighter. The pole bent down. Ted let the reel go and the spool began to unwind with a pleasant, exciting, zinging noise. The trout went upstream for several yards. Leaping and twisting up into the air, then plunging straight down to disappear in a swirl of water. Slowly then, Ted began to put pressure to the line. Gradually the trout's mad speed was lessened, stopped. Gently Ted began to reel in. He let the trout play itself out. Five minutes after the strike he leaned forward, thrust his fingers through the wide-open mouth and gills—and the first battle was over.

But Ted was stumped. He had come off without the tackle box. All he had was a set of trout flies and his pole. How was he going to keep the fish? It would probably spoil if he left it out in the sun. He stood there scratching his head, trying to solve his problem.

"Tenderfeet in trouble? Need Indian Jim?"

"Sa-aay," Ted exclaimed, turning around, "you don't make as much noise as a ghost. But I do need your help. What do I do now that I've got this trout? How do I keep it?"

Jim rubbed his fingernail along the trout's back. "See how slippery fish is?" the red man said. "Slippery outside is trout's protection. It acts like coat—keeps trout from spoiling. Watch Jim." The Indian found several tufts of grass close to the bank. He uprooted them, then dipped them into the stream. He then wrapped the trout in the damp grass, just as you would smother a hot dog inside a bun. With a long strand of bark, he tied the grass about the trout, handed it to Ted. "Grass keep fish fresh. Put in mackinaw pocket and take back to camp."

Ted's luck turned with the catching of his first trout.

Ten minutes after he packed it away in grass in his mackinaw pocket, he had hooked another—this one a shimmering sixteen-inch beauty. Jim followed along behind, silently, approvingly. He would, from time to time, offer Ted a bit of advice.

Once when Ted hooked a fish that looked to be at least twenty inches long, Jim said, "Little fish foot long no have sharp teeth. But big fish like that one have mouth like razor."

"In other words," Ted said, "I don't dare stick my fingers in his mouth—or I might get them snapped off." The Indian nodded and Ted said, "But how would I land him then?"

"Landing net," the Indian said. "Jim show tenderfeet how to make one later on. Right now, catch fish."

But the trout was too smart for the inexperienced Ted. He fought it—but was unable to keep the slack out of the line. The trout leaped high into the air. It seemed to be standing on its tail in the water, shaking its head, snapping at the loose line. The line parted with a snap and the trout went free.

"I don't have to worry about the landing net yet," Ted exclaimed disconsolately. "I messed that up, didn't I. . . ."

Ted suddenly stopped talking. For when he turned around, Jim was gone. The red man had vanished as quietly as he had arrived. It gave Ted a sort of spooky feeling, never knowing when he was alone. On the

other hand, he enjoyed the novelty of it. He liked the
red man's dry humor, liked the way he made pointed
remarks that were so filled with information. It was
almost as if the red man had taken a special liking to
Ted and was doing everything in his power to make
him into a good camper. If that were true, no one was
happier about it than Ted Moran. For Ted, after
getting his first glimpse of the outdoor life, realized
that in order to become proficient in taking care of
himself in the wilderness, it would be necessary to
store up a wealth of knowledge.

He fished until the sun was quite low in the sky. His
catch consisted of six trout, ranging from one to two
pounds in weight. It was a nice catch for a beginner
and Ted was justly proud of his accomplishment. He
wandered back to the starting point and there he found
Pudge, sitting disconsolately upon a rock.

"Well," Pudge said, "I can see where nobody is
going to have to clean fish tonight. You didn't catch
any either. Do you know what? I was fishing along, trying to cast my fly out across the stream, when I hooked
my line over a pine limb on the other bank. All of a
sudden I had a creepy feeling and when I looked
around, there was Indian Jim. Can you beat it? He
just looked at me and said, 'Tenderfeet can't catch
trout in tree.' I worked about thirty seconds more and
then I turned around to ask him where I could get an-

other line. But blotto—he's gone again. I tell you that guy's a ghost."

Ted laughed. He was in a good mood and he said nothing as he unloaded the grass-covered fish from his pockets. Pudge watched him and when all the trout were lying upon a rock, Pudge said suspiciously, "Say, there isn't a fish market up here is there? I can't see how you could get fish and me not get a one."

"Quiet," Ted grinned. "Get to work and get them cleaned before it gets dark. You've got a knife. Get busy. . . ."

Pudge fell laboriously to work. He tugged and wrestled with the first trout. But after he got the grass off the outside, it began to slip in his fingers like a bar of wet soap. The sun went behind the mountain range and the shadows lengthened. Then a long arm reached over Pudge's shoulder. It was Indian Jim again. He took Pudge's knife, thrust the blade through the fish's gills. One slit and the gills were severed. The head then twisted off easily enough. Another slit down the white middle and the insides were exposed. Jim lifted them out, held the trout down in the water. In an instant it was washed and Jim was handing the knife back.

"Much obliged," Pudge said sheepishly. "You make it look easy."

Indian Jim smiled. "Tenderfeet hurry. Jim show how to roast trout on sticks." Although Pudge had lost the contest, Ted fell to work helping him with the fish. In a few moments the job of cleaning them was completed. They followed the Indian up to the flat rock. There were several small campfires glowing. It was now quite dark. The cloak of blackness had descended swiftly, once the sun disappeared. There was something wonderful in the way darkness came—and at the same time, something quite fearful. For, as Ted Moran thought at the time, how much chance would you have if you remained out away from camp until the sun disappeared?

Indian Jim took one of the fish. He found a green branch and with his knife he whittled it to a fine point on the end.

He thrust the stick through the first trout and held it over one of the camp fires. In a moment the trout began to sizzle as the flames hit it. Indian Jim kept turning it until it was a crisp, golden brown.

Ted and Pudge divided the fish. "Say," Pudge exclaimed. "This is the best thing I ever tasted."

They ate trout until they were stuffed. Later they sat around, listening to Jim tell stories of how his ancestors had lived in these same mountains. The hours passed swiftly.

Finally Jeff Jones said, "We're all tired. It's time to get to bed. It's nine o'clock. We have time to carry water to put out the fires and still be in bed in half an hour. Nine-thirty is the deadline and I don't want any-one out after then."

The entire group of young men took their canteens, went down to the stream and filled them. One by one they filed past the fires and emptied the water on them. When they had finished, not a spark remained.

"This is one thing that is always important," Jeff Jones said. "The first law of the camper is to put out all fires. A single spark might start a fire that would rage for days and sweep these mountains clean. The work of years would be undone in minutes. Remember—a fire should never be smothered by dirt. That only keeps it alive. Use water. That's the only way."

Ted and Pudge crawled in under their shelter. They were exceedingly tired and immediately went to sleep. Later—Ted didn't know how long, he heard a move-ment outside and was quickly wide awake. He peered through the flap in his shelter. The moon had come into view beyond the range. What Ted saw was a young man stealing silently toward the stream. A shaft of light fell upon his face, outlining him clearly.

"Rocky Stone . . ." Ted muttered. "And he has his fishing rod with him. Oh—I get it. He thinks fishing would be better at night than in the daytime. Well, it's his business. . . ."

Ted waited, wondering if anyone would awaken to stop Rocky. But the young man was treading silently, proving that he knew his way around in the wilderness. He started down the bank and then suddenly he let out a bloodcurdling scream.

Things happened so swiftly that Ted could not recall later exactly what did occur. He knew that Rocky Stone went crashing through the underbrush, the screams from his lips growing louder and more shrill. The entire camp came awake in startled alarm. And then Ted saw something that turned his own heart to ice. About a hundred feet behind the fleeing Rocky was a huge black animal. The animal was lumbering along at a speed that was incredible. Ted wasn't aware of his own husky whisper . . .

"A bear . . . it's chasing after Rocky. It'll kill him!"

Rocky leaped for a tree, started to climb up it. The bear was in swift pursuit. Instinctively Ted Moran began to run. He was in his thick wool stockings and he ran swiftly and silently. But Ted did not go toward Rocky and the bear. He circled around the entire camp. What was it he had heard about bears? They could climb trees—he was very sure of that. Rocky Stone would be clawed to death if help was not forthcoming.

Ted was at the upper end of the camp. Now he leaped down the embankment to the stream. In the moonlight he soon located the tin boxes that contained the provisions. He picked the largest one, tore the lid off. Inside he found a large piece of fresh beef. Ted clambered back up the bank, beef in hand. When he reached the camp again, he discovered that half the campers were up. Flash beams were stabbing the air. Some of the fellows were shouting. Some of them were remaining in their tents, hoping the bear would not turn on them. Someone was shining a light into the tree the hapless Rocky had climbed. The bear by now was pawing its way up the branches.

Ted raced out almost to the tree. He climbed to the top of a rock about ten feet from the tree. Aiming carefully, he threw the bloody piece of meat at the bear. He scored a direct hit on the bear's nose. And that was all Mr. Bear wanted with Rocky Stone. The bear snapped at the meat, caught it. In a moment the animal beat a hasty retreat into the woods, the fresh meat locked tightly in its jaws.

There was a burst of spontaneous cheering. As for Ted, he just sat down weakly. Now that it was over, he wondered how he had ever gone through with it. How he had ever been able to ignore the bear as it growled those ominous warnings.

"That was fine work, Ted Moran," Jeff Jones exclaimed.

"I . . . I happened to remember what you said in the meeting yesterday—about bears liking fresh meat, I mean. That was the only thing I could think of to do."

"That was enough to think of," the camp director exclaimed. "I think a certain young man owes you a vote of thanks."

Rocky Stone, for the first time since Ted had known him, looked entirely subdued. He came forward sheepishly. "Thanks," he said. Then he dived for the tent and made no more noise.

6. CRAZY OLD MAN OF THE MOUNTAINS

FOR a week after the bear scare, the campers remained close to their cabins. Most of their time was spent in fishing in the large lake below the camp site. The reason for this was simple.

The award for the largest fish caught during the camp period was one hundred points. By now the forthcoming point award contest was a subject of heated conversation and more than one young hopeful went to sleep each night, dreaming of a gold star emblem for himself and a check for fifty thousand dollars for his school.

Ted Moran had spent every extra moment on the lake, trying to bag a large trout. But by the end of the week he hadn't even gotten into the race. A fellow named Rex Lawrence had landed a four-pound German Brown trout. That looked large enough to place high in the contest—perhaps win it.

But Ted was not giving up. One afternoon he and Pudge got into a canoe and decided to hit out for the north end of the lake. The distance was about a mile from camp and after a stiff paddle, they reached the shore line.

"Maybe this is the day I can hook into that old rascal I met the first day out," Ted said. He tied on one of his brightest flies. But several casts failed to produce as much as a small strike. Ted changed flies and tried again, but to no avail. For more than two hours he flipped his line into the likely-looking little inlets, but not a strike did he get. Rounding a small jutting rock ledge, they came upon half a dozen other boats.

"Say, are you fellows doing any good?" Ted shouted. "I've fished all over this end of the lake and haven't had a strike."

Rex Lawrence, the young man who was leading the fishing derby, recognized Ted. "The trout aren't biting at all today. We've stopped fishing altogether. Right now we're debating about something. Look, Moran, do you see that shack up there at the edge of the clearing. See, it's right through there. . . ."

There was a rickety-looking stone shack from which a thin column of smoke was pouring. Ted thought that curious. "I had the idea that not a living person could be found for miles around. I wonder how long that has been there? Who could be living there anyway? A hermit?"

Rex Lawrence sobered. "I've been fishing over here every day. I've seen the old guy who lives there. He has a beard and goes around with only an old pair of trousers and an undershirt. I've watched him dozens of times. He's crazy, I tell you. He's always digging around—must be searching for gold. I've nicknamed him the Old Prospector. Right now we're wondering if we should go up there and look his place over."

Ted was immediately interested. "That might be a good idea," he said. "But what about this fellow being crazy? If that's the case, I'd think you'd be running a strong chance. If he owns the property and you trespass, you can't tell what he might do. However, if you're going—count me in."

Ted and Pudge joined a small group. They tied their boat beside a small dock, noticing that another boat was tied there. This one, Ted decided, must belong to the Old Prospector.

They topped a rise, being careful not to make any noise. The old man wasn't in sight. They were almost up to the cabin's door now. Rex Lawrence said, "You can see here where he has been digging. Look at those ditches, would you. Just holes in the ground." Rex Lawrence jumped down into one of them, bent over. "If there's anything here that looks like gold, I'll eat it. Look around you guys. See if I'm crazy. . . ."

That was all Rex Lawrence had time to say. For suddenly the door of the cabin burst open. Ted Moran saw it all and he was as surprised—as frightened—as the rest. For it was evident at once that there was such a personage as the Old Prospector. He bolted from the door of the cabin. He was a small, slender-looking man. But he was aged. He had a gray beard and wild-looking eyes that were set deeply in their sockets. His hair and his beard waved in the light breeze as he came toward them, waving his arms wildly, shouting loudly.

"Get out of there. Get out of that ditch. Oh, you've ruined my precious treasures. Get out, I say. Get out!"

The man was advancing. Rex Lawrence let out a scream. He dived out of the ditch, rolled over and over, came to his feet and began to run. Ted Moran, having seen the whole thing in the flash of an eye, was of the conclusion that the old man really was crazy. Crazier, perhaps, than Rex Lawrence had imagined him to be. For the old man had mentioned that his precious treasures were ruined. There was nothing precious about solid rock, Ted concluded. So Ted Moran decided it was time to leave. He headed for the edge of the lake where the boats were waiting. The old man was in hot pursuit. He was screaming at the top of his lungs, but no one tried to understand him.

Ted was the last to reach his canoe. He leaped to safety, and Pudge, who had a paddle in his hand, began to paddle furiously. They were about fifty feet from the dock when the Old Prospector leaped toward his own boat—and then, tripping, plunged into the water.

"Haw. Lookit. The old guy's in the water. Maybe

that'll soak some of the crazy ideas out of his head. Haw, haw . . ."

It did look funny. The old man was splashing around, waving his arms wildly, shouting at the top of his lungs. Ted laughed along with the rest of them— and his laugh then froze in his throat. For he saw that despite the loud shoutings, the old man was in serious trouble. His head kept bobbing and each time it came up, he was visibly more feeble. "Wait . . . Pudge, turn around. The Old Prospector's really drowning. I've got to help him . . ."

Pudge sat there dazed. Ted, without waiting to argue, stood up in the canoe, ripped his mackinaw off. He was wearing rubber boots and he kicked out of them easily. In a twinkling he launched his muscled young body through the air in a clean dive. His fingers hit the water, cleaved it. He entered the water easily. The first cold shock was like jumping into a snow bank. But it soon passed. By the time Ted came up to the surface again, he had gotten over the shock. He had also gotten ten feet closer to the old man. He heard a frantic shout—but this was from the other direction. He heard Rex Lawrence's voice.

"Keep away from him, Ted. He's crazy. He'll drown you."

Ted Moran saw a man drowning. It did not matter now that the man was crazy. The fact that a human life was endangered was enough to keep him driving through the water.

Ted approached the old man. He could see the wild, maniacal gleam in his eyes. A frenzied gleam that is in the eye of every drowning man. Long, talon-like fingers reached out avidly, clutched at Ted. Ted knew that once those fingers were sunk into him, he might be strangled to death before he could tear loose. For he knew the amazing strength of a drowning man.

Three feet in front of the man, Ted dived. He went down about five feet. He opened his eyes and with a sun still shining down from overhead, it was easy enough to see. He swam forward until he reached the old man's knees. Then putting his hands on the old man's knees, he gave him a quick turn around. Ted was now behind the man. He came up swiftly and before the old man could clutch at him, Ted hooked his fingers in the long hair, pulled the man over on his back and began to swim toward the shore. The old man fought for a time, but on his back, he was unable to reach Ted. Suddenly he went limp and Ted had no more trouble. He lifted the unconscious old man to the bank. By that time the other campers had gotten over their shock and were now rowing frantically toward Ted.

But he paid them no heed. His mind was recalling everything he had learned about lifesaving. He laid the old man down on the ground, folded his arm under his face and turned his head sideways, resting it on the arm. Ted looked to see that the old fellow's tongue hadn't been swallowed—he knew that this sometimes happened in drownings—then immediately set to work.

He straddled the Old Prospector and then, putting his hands in the small of his back, began to pump rhythmically in an effort to induce breathing. He repeated a little poem he had learned so that his timing would be correct. As he pushed down, he said, "Out goes the bad air. . . ." Then taking his weight off the man's back, he added, "In comes the good. . . . ."

Ted kept that up. "Out goes the bad air. In comes the good." He saw the old man's color begin to change from blue-black to a flesh tint. Rex Lawrence, leaning over Ted, said, "He'll come out of it now. You'd better beat it while you have a chance. You can't tell what the crazy old coot will do."

"No . . . no, this man needs care. But perhaps it would be a good idea if you fellows left. A lot of us around might disturb him. Pudge, you go back to camp with Lawrence. I'll keep the canoe and I can come on along when I get him taken care of."

Pudge looked doubtful. But he had long ago learned that when Ted Moran made a decision, he kept it, regardless of what anyone else thought. So with a few apprehensive backward glances, he departed with the rest.

Ted was inclined to feel a bit apprehensive himself.

But he needn't have. For when the Old Prospector came out of it, he was as gentle as a lamb. He looked up at Ted, blinked his small eyes quickly. They were shrewd eyes that were sharp and probing.

"Say, young fellow, I can't understand why you didn't let me drown. I heard what your friends said—called me a crazy old galoot. Well, maybe I am. Maybe I ain't got any sense at all. But I have fun. Yes sir, I reckon if a man wants to spend his time diggin' in the ground, that's his business. Now you take me—I like to dig. Get a big kick out of it. Some folks might say I'm crazy. I say I'm not. What do you say, young man?"

Ted considered the thing from every angle. "Well— a man has a right to his own choice. And certainly, you can't be accused of talking like a crazy man. But look, Prospector, you just had a close call. I think we'd better go inside and get you into some warm clothes. For that matter, I'd like to dry out my own clothes . . ."

The old man was visibly weak as Ted helped him inside. They entered the cabin which was a small, one-room affair. It was crudely furnished. There was a stove and a bunk and an old rickety chair. Nothing else— except a pile of rocks in one corner. But the place was clean and that was a good sign.

The old man offered Ted a blanket and Ted, after hanging his clothes over the chair, wrapped the blanket around him. He put the Prospector to bed. "What you need is some hot soup," Ted said. "And I'm the fellow that can fix it."

But Ted was in for a surprise. When he looked in the small cupboard, he found nothing but a few crusts of bread and some bacon.

Ted felt a swift stab of embarrassment. He knew then that the Old Prospector must be desperately poor. He tried to hide his feelings, but the old man said, "I know what you're thinkin'. You can't find anything to eat. Well, the truth is, I did run out of provisions. But I'll have more."

Ted warmed toward the old fellow. He realized, of course, that the Old Prospector had his pride—that he hated to admit that he was without food or funds.

The Prospector looked at Ted shrewdly. "Young man, you saved my life. But even if you hadn't—well, I think I'd like you for the way you figure things out. Take me, for instance. I'm supposed to be dangerous. Everybody else leaves me alone. But you—well, you decide for yourself that I'm harmless, so you pay me a visit. That's the way to learn things, son. Be curious. And don't be afraid. Now who can tell—maybe I can teach you things that you've never heard of. Me, I live in the woods. I know about the forests and streams and mountains. You come back and see me again when you get a chance. Never can tell. We might get to be fast friends. . . ." The old man cocked a quizzical eye and for a moment, that eye fairly twinkled. "Unless," he said softly, "you're afraid to be friendly with a crazy man."

Ted suddenly grinned. "My clothes are about dry," he said, "and I have to get back to camp, anyway. But I'll tell you one thing before I leave. I'm a tenderfoot and I have a lot to learn. But there's a fish in this lake— a big one. Brown Beauty. I have a special reason for wanting to catch him. Some time, if you don't mind, I wish you'd show me how."

Ted got ready to leave and the Prospector got up out of bed, followed him to the door. "I owe you a favor, youngster. And by cracky, I'm going to repay it. If there's one thing I know, it's fishin'. I've tangled with Brown Beauty myself. Heaps of times. I've never landed him but I know the old coot's weaknesses. If it's the last thing I do, I'm going to show you how to get him."

Ted wrung the old man's hand. "You're crazy," he whispered softly, "you're crazy—like a fox. Well, good-by, Prospector. I'll be dropping in to take that lesson."

But back at camp Ted received a setback. After the meal he was called into the office of Jeff Jones. Rex Lawrence and the others who had been there that after-noon were also present.

"Fellows," Jeff Jones said, "I heard about your ex-ploit this afternoon. Personally, I don't like it. I've heard tales of this fellow you call the Prospector. But

I haven't investigated him. He owns his land and he keeps to himself. But from what I hear, he should be kept away from. You young men are here at camp in my care. I can't allow you to take any chances. If you go over there again, you can't tell what will happen to you. Therefore, I'm forbidding anyone in camp from setting foot on the other side of the lake. I hate to be strict—but after all, I'm expected to protect you while you're here."

"I understand exactly," Ted Moran said. "But in this case, I think we're all being unfair with Prospector. I spent a part of the afternoon with him. He's a nice old fellow. I halfway promised him that I'd be back to see him and I'd like to keep my promise."

The camp director looked disappointed. "Sorry, Moran. The fact that nothing happened to you today is no sign that you'll be as fortunate in the future. I must warn you again—keep away from the far shore of the lake. That's all."

The group broke up. As for Ted, he hated the turn things had taken. He wanted to pay another visit to Old Prospector—and yet, how could he?

"You act insulted," Pudge complained. "I can't understand why you would want to spend your time with a crazy man."

"Old Prospector isn't crazy," Ted said softly. "He's smart. A lot smarter than you think. I try to follow rules, Pudge. But between you and me, this one is going to be hard to keep. I'm right—and when I'm right, you know that I take chances . . ."

"Now wait a minute, Paul Revere. Don't ride off in the dark. Do you realize that when you talk that way, you're risking a grandstand for Tech? Are you crazy too?"

"Sometimes," Ted said savagely, "I think so . . . ."

7. SONG OF DANGER

TED MORAN didn't get a chance to call on Old Prospector—at least not for awhile. For an unusually late
storm descended on the eastern slope one evening and
when the camp dug out in the morning, it was under
a foot of snow. The snow was accompanied by a cold
wave and simply wouldn't melt. The campers spent the
first day skiing down the slopes. That evening Jerry
Severns, the ranger of that district, came into camp.
After conferring with the camp director for awhile,
he reappeared in the lounge. Jeff Jones asked for silence and when he got it, he turned the meeting over
to the young forest ranger.

"Men," the ranger said, "this snow has covered the
mountains and most of the natural feed has been covered. If the cold keeps up for as long as a week, I'm
afraid there will be trouble. There are hundreds of
wolves in the forests. With their food all covered by
snow, the wolves are going to move down the slopes.
Below here are several large sheep ranches. Wolves kill

sheep. My idea is to organize a gigantic wolf hunt—in case the cold weather holds. I'm pleased to learn that this idea would tie in quite well with your program here."

There was a round of enthusiastic applause. Wolf hunting had all the appeal to such a group as a circus would have had to fellows ten years younger.

Jeff Jones took over for a moment, "Fellows, you realize that one hundred points will be given to the best hunter. Most hunting in the mountains is done in the winter time. This snow, however, gives us an excellent opportunity to have our hunting contest now. So I've decided to make this hunt official. The camper who makes the best showing on the wolf hunt will receive first points. Now since we won't be going out for a few days—and perhaps, if the snow does not melt at all—we will have sufficient time to train for the occasion. The first thing of course is to learn something about rifle shooting.

"Colonel Cassiday has provided rifles for everyone and tomorrow morning, we'll begin to practice with them. Right now I want to give you a few pointers. A rifle is a dangerous weapon, but an effective one. There is one thing to remember. Never fire at a moving object until you know what it is. For heaven's sake, when a bush moves, hold your fire—for it might turn out to be some of your friends instead of an animal. You will discover that your rifle has a device near the trigger, called a safety catch. Keep this on. That will keep your rifle from going off in case you fall to the ground or hit the gun against a tree or rock. There is plenty of time to take the safety off when you do see the game. There are other things to remember, but they can come later. Right now I imagine you are interested in learning more about wolves. I'll let Jerry tell you."

Once again the young forest ranger took charge. "A wolf," he said, "is a dangerous animal. A wolf is a coward, generally. But when one is aroused, when one is hungry—beware. Wolves can rip you to shreds with their huge claws. They can sink their deadly fangs into the throat of a human being so swiftly that you haven't a chance to defend yourself. It has been said that a wolf will not attack a person—but don't you believe it. Don't get the idea that I am trying to frighten you. With firearms and clear thinking, you should all be able to hold your own. My purpose in telling you all this is so that you will not get the idea that you are going off on a picnic. There will be danger every inch of the way. But I'm sure you'll experience so many thrills that you won't mind the dangerous aspects. Well, fellows, that's about all. Get those rifles out tomorrow and get in some good practice. If this cold holds out, the wolves will be down the slopes and the hunt will be on . . . ."

The ranger had given a clear enough description of mountain wolves. But three nights later every camper knew from a much more vivid source, exactly how chilling the presence of wolves could be. For that night another snow began. A fine, sifting snow that was like dry powder. About midnight there was a long ghostly wailing sound from the south of the camp. Almost immediately there came another wail—this one from another direction.

From the first piercing wail, the word went through the cabins. "Wolves. The wolves are coming down!"

Ted Moran and Pudge Lawson were only two of the dozens of campers who got up that night. Flashlights were discreetly turned on and now and then when a piercing call rang through the timber, when it seemed that the wolf must be almost upon the camp, one of the campers would flash his light in that direction.

"Br-rr-rrr!" Pudge exclaimed. "This is something that chills your blood, even with a stove going full blast." The two friends were gazing out the south window of the cabin. Suddenly the very breath seemed to freeze up in Ted's throat, then surge forth in a husky hissing sound.

"I'll show you something that will chill your blood. Look off toward that tree. See those eyes—they look like two green traffic lights. It's a wolf, Pudge. Just in the edge of the clearing. Watch. I'm going to flip on my flash." Ted pointed the flashlight in the direction of the eyes, turned it on. Suddenly the snow was illuminated in a brilliant glow and there, standing like a large, overgrown police dog, was a wolf. At the sight

of the light, the wolf bared his fangs, growled men-
acingly, then like the coward it was, turned and beat
a hasty retreat into the timber.

"That means our hunt is a cinch," Ted said. "If we
expect to get out early, we'll have to sleep—if we can
sleep with a pack of wolves howling in our ears."

Sleep they did, although their slumbers were punc-
tuated by the wailings of packs of roving wolves. At
dawn they were out of their beds and ready to take to
the woods at the first signal. Their rifles were well
oiled and all of them had sufficient ammunition to last
a day. Shortly after breakfast, Jerry, the ranger, put
in his appearance. He was carrying a rifle under his
arm and upon his face was a look of eagerness.

"Last night's snow made it all the better," he told
the campers. "We'll have plenty of sport. Now here's
the way we'll work it. From here we'll spread out fan-
wise. Because of the fresh snow, every man will make
new footprints. If you follow this one rule you can't
possibly get lost. Don't cross anyone else's tracks. When
you get as far as you want to go, turn around and follow your tracks back to camp. I would suggest that you
go off in groups of two or three. And remember—
wolves are dangerous. This won't be easy."

Ted and Pudge had been standing off at the edge of
the group. Ted said, "Come on, Pudge. Let's go out
and get them."

But Pudge didn't take a step. "Listen, Ted," the

heavy youngster said seriously, "I'm too slow at this business to do you any good. There's a hundred points in prospect for the winner of the event. If I tag along, I'll slow you down."

"Oh, don't be a pessimist," Ted exclaimed. "Come on."

"I'm talking sense, you thickheaded mule, and you know it. I've been watching Rocky Stone in practice. He's a dead shot. Besides he takes to this snow and he'll cover a lot of territory. Use your head and start out with him—look, he's edging over this way. He must have the same idea about it."

Rocky Stone was indeed coming toward them. His dark face was twisted in an insolent smirk. "Well, dead-eye," he said, "I guess you think you can outshoot any guy in these mountains. I'd like to give you a little example of how to really hunt wolves. How'd you like to wander along with me?"

"What you want," Pudge interrupted hotly, "is to be sure that you get a shot before Ted does. You figure if you go with him that you can keep him from getting those points . . . ."

"Quiet, Pudge," Ted snapped. "Of course, I'll go with Rocky."

The two young rivals for the gold star honor left the clearing and entered the timber. The snow of the night before had covered all tracks so Ted didn't be-

lieve it would be possible to track any of the wolves—
unless they should happen to run onto fresh tracks
that had been made after the snow had stopped falling.

They walked for half an hour in silence. It was
Rocky Stone who spoke first: "I suppose you've done a
lot of hunting, Moran."

Ted Moran said quietly, "As a matter of fact, the
only thing I've hunted before is rabbits. This is all new
to me."

The taller Rocky grinned indulgently. "If we get
into trouble, I'll get you out of it. Lucky you came
along with me. This is old stuff as far as I'm concerned.
Why, I've hunted lots of things before. Bear? Why I've
brought down dozens of them."

Ted didn't say anything. There was no doubting the
fact that Rocky was a crack shot with his rifle. For in
rifle practice during the earlier part of the week, Rocky
had consistently hit the bull's-eye while Ted had had
to practice long hard hours before he could control his
shots.

They passed through the timbered area and emerged
on a steep, rocky slope. The rocks were well-covered
with snow. Some of them were as large as houses, while
others were quite small. But the thing that impressed
Ted was that beneath many of them there were small
pockets that no snow had been able to reach. These
cavelike places impressed him as being good shelter for

animals—for wolves. So Ted began to pay particular attention to those places. Noon came and still they had had no luck.

They reached a large rock. The north side was covered by a huge snow drift. The south side was only sparsely covered. Rocky suggested that they stop there and eat the lunches they had brought. Ted was in agreement. But first he decided he would have a look around the south side of that rock. He stepped in and out of smaller crevices, made his way around to the south face of the boulder. The first thing he saw was a set of fresh tracks. They looked like the tracks of a huge dog.

The glare of the snow had partially blinded him. Now he stood there, peering back in under the rock. It was rather dark. But before Ted could become used to the darkness, trouble was upon him. He heard the chilling wolf snarl, the low, throaty gurgle that has paralyzed so many hunters with cold fear. And then a white, tan-tinted body was hurtling through the air at him. In a split second Ted Moran realized his plight. He had stumbled upon a den. How many wolves were there, he didn't know. But he did know one thing. He was gazing into the dripping jaws of death. Instinct alone was all that saved Ted. He saw that he would not be able to shoot. So he dived to the ground. The wolf was already in the middle of its leap and it was impossible for it to change course. So when Ted fell

face forward, the wolf sailed over him. But one sharp
claw had reached out, had found Ted's range. Ted felt
a searing pain across his shoulders. He knew, of course,
that his clothes had been ripped by the steel-like claw.
And he felt the stabbing ache in his body. How badly
he had been clawed, he hadn't the slightest idea. He
saw the wolf land beyond him. Ted leaped to his feet,
picked up his rifle and swinging it from the barrel, he
found that it made an effective club. The next time
the wolf leaped, he swung hard and the wooden stock
hit the animal in the side of the head. The wolf went
down in the snow, dead.

But Ted did not realize that his danger was just beginning. He heard another wolfish growl behind him.
This time when he turned around, there were two
wolves. Big, angry-looking fellows, attracted to him,
no doubt, by the loud scuffling and the unmistakable
scent of blood. For as Ted turned around, he saw the
pink spot on the light snow. A pink spot that grew
wider by the moment. Ted knew it was from his own
injury.

The wolves charged him together. Ted stood there,
swinging his gun, fighting them off. His first swing hit
one wolf in the side, knocked it into the other. Both
animals went down in a tangled ball of tawny fur. Ted
backed up half a dozen steps before they arose to charge
him again. Once again Ted was able to beat them off.
Now, he was out into the clear. He swung his gun

around. His thumb found the safety button. He pushed it off, swung the gun up to his shoulder just as the twin terrors attacked again. But this time there came two sharp spats of rifle fire. Lead whined through the air. The wolves fell dead. Ted looked up above him, in the direction from which the shots had come. Rocky Stone, the big brave game hunter who believed that it was better to stand still and use your head than to run when attacked, had taken refuge on the top of the rock. He was standing there, holding his smoking gun.

"Well," Rocky said triumphantly, "I saved your life. On top of that, I bagged two wolves. That ought to be good for a hundred points, don't you think?"

Inside, Ted knew that Rocky had not saved his life. Had he decided to run as Rocky did, both of them would probably have been clawed to death. And as for Rocky getting credit for two kills, well, that was hard to take. But the fact remained that technically, Rocky had killed two animals while Ted had killed only one. So there was nothing for him to do but take it as graciously as possible.

"Yes . . . yes, I imagine that it would be enough to get the hunting points, all right. But I'm still not going to give up. I have an idea. But first take a look at my back, will you? It's clawed and with that hole in my mackinaw, it's pretty breezy."

Rocky examined the wound. "It's a long scratch,"

he said, "but it isn't very deep. A little iodine on it and you'll get along all right. Maybe you'd better go back to camp."

"And leave you out here all by yourself to possibly add more to your total," Ted said drily. "Not a chance. I'm staying until I get another shot or two. Well, come on. The only way we can prove we got wolves at all is to cut off their ears and carry them back to camp. That's easier than packing the wolves back."

They advanced upon their game, snipped off the ears with their long bladed hunting knives. The sight of the animal blood gave Ted another idea. "Look," he said. "The wind is blowing down from the north. If we get north of these dead wolves, the scent of blood will probably be stronger than the human scent. If there are any more hungry wolves, they'll be coming this way to investigate. That might give us another chance to add to our scores." Ted saw the appreciative light in Rocky Stone's eyes and he knew what Rocky was thinking. "I might remind you," Ted added, "that the idea is mine. Therefore, I get the first shot in case anything comes along."

Rocky didn't say anything. They went back up on the rock and began to eat their lunches. Suddenly without saying a word, Rocky lifted his rifle and fired. Ted looked around and saw a wolf lying dead in the snow. He also saw another one bounding toward shelter. He lifted his own rifle, aimed carefully down the sights.

When the sights were pointed at the wolf's head, he fired. The wolf took two more steps, then tumbled over, lay still.

"I thought," Ted said, "that I was to get the first shot. I could have killed both of them easily enough."

"I was afraid," Rocky commented, "that if I opened my mouth to tell you they were approaching, they might hear me and turn around and get away. It was too good a chance to pass up."

Ted was, for the first time in his life, so angry that he could think of nothing to say. He liked to follow the code of fair play. He knew he had been taken advantage of and yet because it was his nature to make the best of every situation, no matter how unbearable, he decided it would be just as well to keep quiet. The damage was done. His score was two and Rocky had killed three.

They remained there throughout the greater part of the afternoon. The sun came out and because it was June the snow began to melt swiftly. By late afternoon no other game had appeared. Ted saw their vanishing footprints behind them. He knew that before long it would be possible for them to lose their way back to camp. He suggested that they leave and this met with instant approval from Rocky.

The trip back to camp was accomplished without incident. It was dusk when they finally came to the Administration Building. Most of the other hunters were already in. Several were relating the narrow escapes they had had but when Ted's wound was exhibited, they crowded around him and demanded to hear of his experience. He recounted it quietly and modestly and when he came to the part Rocky had played in the affair, he was careful to give Rocky credit for good shooting. He did not mention his own ideas on the affair. Thus Rocky was elevated to the rank of temporary camp hero. Rocky's three sets of ears were enough to win for him the first points. That night, the score went up on the board. Six campers had bagged one wolf each and all of them were tied for third. But it was the first points that interested Ted. And Rocky had them. The score was Rocky: 100. Ted: 50.

8. PROSPECTOR PAYS OFF

AFTER the unseasonal snow in mid-June, the weather cleared and the sun began to shine every day. The days were brilliant blazing periods when every camper liked to be out of doors. Ted and Pudge spent every waking hour, either in the forest or on the lake. They fished much of the time, but Ted was never able to hook into anything larger than a three-pound rainbow trout. He was beginning to wonder if he would have a chance at all in the gold star point award contest. Those hundred points of Rocky Stone's loomed larger and larger. To make matters even more difficult, Ted received a letter from his dad.

"Dear Son," his dad had written, "I have heard from Pudge Lawson's mother that you are in a contest. According to Pudge, you have a fighting chance of winning. I do not know too much of the nature of the events, but I would imagine that they have to do with the forest and streams. If this is so, I believe I can give you some good advice. Keep your eyes and ears open. When someone from the mountains starts to speak, you would do well to listen. I have been in the mountains several times myself. Once I met a man who was a sheepherder. He had never been out of the hills and he could hardly speak a word of correct grammar. But he was wealthy in experience.

"He made fires without matches. He could find his way home from anywhere, simply by knowing how to make trail. He made his own clothing out of skins, took care of his health when there were no doctors within miles.

"I am telling you this, Ted, because I know that you are the kind who takes advantage of every given opportunity. Perhaps in your section, there is an old rancher, or sheepherder or someone who would like to teach an eager young man something about woodcraft. This is just an idea, but it might be something for you to think about. Well, I have written enough for this time. I wish you luck in your contest. You know that I am pulling for you at all times. Most affectionately, Dad."

That letter made it difficult for Ted because he could read between the lines just how strongly his father wanted him to win. And being like most parents, the elder Moran had implicit faith in his own son. He believed Ted to be capable of anything he set his mind to accomplishing. There were no ifs, ands or buts about it. Ted had to win that award!

There was one thing, however, that Ted did get

from the letter. That was the point about learning from those who knew. Indian Jim had been a very valuable friend and at times he had talked for hours with Ted. But the trouble with Jim was that he was supposed to take care of all of the boys. Thus his time was so divided that no one person could expect to learn everything from him. There was one man, however, who did know some of the things Ted wanted to learn. That man was Old Prospector.

Ted really tried to obey orders. But the next time he climbed into his canoe alone, he found himself drifting toward the far shore of the lake. He kept telling himself that his real purpose was to try to tie into the famous old trout, Brown Beauty. But deep down in his heart he knew differently. He was hoping to see Old Prospector again.

Ted drifted closer and closer to the old man's boat dock. He was casting his line into the likely-looking spots, but his heart was not on fishing and he knew it. He glanced up toward Old Prospector's shack. The place did not look deserted for the door was half open and a thin spiral of smoke was curling up from the stone chimney. Then listening carefully, Ted heard the scraping sound that metal makes when it bangs against rock.

Looking off to the right, he saw the Prospector, stripped to the waist, his upper body the color of old copper under the blazing June sun, standing in the center of a hole. He was laboriously tossing dirt and rocks out of it. But when he sighted Ted, he stopped digging and climbed up to the level of the ground.

"Hello, me hearty," he shouted. "Thought you'd forgot the Old Prospector ever lived here. Or maybe," he said slyly, cocking an eye at Ted, "maybe you thought I was crazy after all. Like right now, for instance, digging out here in this hot sun like this. Come on, now, youngster—what kept you away?"

Ted could not help himself then. He pulled into the dock and made no effort to pull away as the Prospector walked toward him. "It does look queer," he said, "the way you're always digging. Surely you don't expect to find gold around here."

"No . . . I know better. There's half a dozen mine shafts up in the mountains close to here. Never was more than a trace o' gold dug out. I reckon I won't ever strike gold. I ain't lookin' for it, though. No, son, I'm one of them pesky old men who just likes to dig up things. Get a big kick out of it. Keeps me healthy and out of doors. I reckon that stamps me as a lunatic to some—but I'm an old man and I'm still able to kick around."

There was logic in what Old Prospector said. Lots of logic. Ted suddenly began to hope that when he was as old as Prospector he would be as healthy, that he would be able to have as much fun as Prospector seemed to be having.

"The reason I haven't been to see you," Ted said slowly, "is that I'm busy. You see we're having a contest over there. It may not mean much to you but to me it's everything. You said once that you'd be glad to teach me anything you knew about the forest and streams."

"Aye, I did, youngster. And when I make a promise, I keep it. Get out of that canoe now and tell me all about it. And, confidentially," the Prospector said, lowering his voice, "tell me—did they make you promise to stay away from here? Ah, you needn't answer that one. I can see you turning red. Well, I don't blame them much. They probably think I am crazy from all the tales they've heard. But what about you? What will happen to you if you get caught over here?"

Ted wrinkled his forehead in a thoughtful frown. "I don't know, sir. I . . . I like to follow orders, but this time, I simply can't. I like you and I know I'm not doing wrong when I visit with you. When I know that I'm right about a thing—well, I'm willing to take chances on going ahead, that's all. So in this case, I'm going to visit you when I feel like it and if anything happens to me for it, I'll just have to like it."

"That's the old spirit," Prospector said. "Know your own mind. Make your own decisions. That's the only way."

Ted got out of his canoe, tied it to the dock. Then he followed Prospector up to his cabin. The old man put on a shirt, handed Ted a small hatchet, took one for himself and said, "Come on, sonny, you and I are going out into the woods for the rest of the day. If it's things about the forest you want to know, the old Prospector can teach you. While we walk, I guess we can talk. If there's anything special, just ask questions."

Ted found it easy to talk to the old man. For instance, he was soon discussing the gold star qualifications. "I could still even the score with Rocky Stone —he's the fellow I'm worried most about—if I could score first in trapping or fishing or woodcraft. But I don't know. We haven't said much about trapping yet. I don't know how they're planning to work the contest. Besides, what could a person trap up here?"

"I guess it'd be easier to tell you what you couldn't trap, young feller. There's bears, lots of them. And lions and more wolves than you could shake a stick at. Funny thing about them, though. The bigger and more dangerous they are, the harder they are to catch. Take a bear for instance. There's an animal that's cunning. It takes a wise hunter to shoot him and an even wiser trapper to trap him. You've got to outsmart old Mr. Bruin—or he makes a fool out of you. There's more to it than just setting a trap. You've got to put the trap where the bear will be.

"What's more, you've got to hide the trap so well that it doesn't look suspicious. Many's the time I have seen bears walk up to traps and sniff all around them without stepping into them. They get suspicious and then there's no catching them at all. The best bet is to find where a wild animal makes its den. If you can get a trap in there while the animal is gone, well, you've got a good chance to taste bear meat. But see here, there's not a chance of anyone in that camp trapping a bear. They haven't the time or patience. Somebody might catch a wolf some night—but not a bear."

They walked through what seemed to be miles of forest. Every now and then the Old Prospector would swing his hatchet and a nick of bark would fly out of a tree.

Finally Ted said, "Why are you doing that, Prospector?"

The old man smiled. "I was waitin' for you to wake up and ask that question. You see, when I make a mark on a tree, the mark looks fresh. I take a hundred steps ahead and then I make another mark. That way I know where I'm goin'. Look, suppose we was to get lost right now. I'd mark this spot right here with a pile of rocks. Then I'd step off a hundred paces in the direction I thought I came from. Pretty soon I'd find one of those trees with the mark. Then, I'd look in the direction of the other mark and that way I'd be able to locate the next one. If you're walkin' in one direction, you always make your mark point the way you're goin'. That way it's pretty hard to lose yourself. If you get lost, the next best thing is to hunt for a stream.

Follow the stream, because in the mountains you can be sure that every little stream eventually empties into a larger one. Sooner or later you'll bump into a cabin or a watering place for stock."

"Is it true," Ted asked, "that the way to tell north is by looking at the trees? I've heard that moss grows on the north side of trees only."

"You hear a lot of things," Prospector commented drily, "but they're not true. Moss is apt to grow anywhere. Look at that tree over there. It has moss all around it—main reason is because it's always damp in that spot. There's lots of other ways of markin' a trail. One way is with stones. Take a long flat stone and point it in a certain direction and about a hundred yards ahead put another stone out in plain sight. When you turn, change the direction of your pointed stones. If you're in timber country where there are a lot of small saplings, cut through a sapling. When it falls, point it in the direction of your trail. Say, I'll tell you about a game I used to play with the Indians. 'Twas fun. We'll play it, by gumbo.

"Look, I'm gonna start across country. I'll mark a plain trail. I want to see if you've learned enough to follow it. Just remember what I've told you and you won't have too much trouble. And don't bother about gettin' lost. If you get more than a hundred yards beyond one of the trail markers I leave, stop and wait. I'll double back and find you. How about it?"

Ted Moran's blood was beginning to tingle, just as it always did when excitement was in the offing. "Nothing," he said, "could be better. The sooner you start, the sooner the fun begins."

Ted sat down to wait. He waited for perhaps ten minutes. He realized that he was far from camp and that his skill would be put to a strict test.

Finally he started out. The Prospector had started off to Ted's left, so Ted began to walk in that direction. He kept his eyes open and soon he came to the first sign—a small sapling that had been cut through in one stroke. It was leaning toward a huge granite boulder. Ted sighted down the fallen trunk, then began to go in the direction it had pointed. He covered his hundred steps and stopped. Nothing appeared that he could take for a marker. He had passed out of the trees and was in a rock-strewn flat place. He turned around and walked back to the fallen sapling. Once again he started out. This took him back to the identical spot. He looked around suddenly, disappointed. Was he to fail before he even got started?

And then he saw it. Upon a flat dry rock was a smaller rock. This rock was damp. Ted looked around and he saw a place where the rock had been lifted from the damp clay. His reasoning told him that a wet rock could not have been there long. The old Prospector was giving him a stiff test. The wet rock pointed off to the right at a sharp angle. Ted followed it and

although he was often stumped, he always went back
to the last marker and started over. Sometimes the trail
was marked by fallen saplings, other times by rocks or
nicks in dead trees. But when the afternoon was half
over, he was still on the trail. He rounded a jutting
rock and suddenly came upon the old Prospector. The
old man was sitting down, resting.

"You learn fast, youngster. It's all I could do to keep
ahead of you. We've been circlin' most of the time.
We've covered about six miles, but we're less than half
a mile from my cabin so we can take a short cut home.
Come on—I reckon these old legs of mine have had
enough for one day."

"Prospector—what's that? That large hole over
there?"

"Oh, that?" the Prospector laughed, "Why that's
a mine shaft. Remember my telling about gold mines
not being any good around here? Well, that's one that
wasn't. They spent a lot of money digging but never
got much for their pains—'cept a lot of blisters. That's
a deep mine, too, I hear. But I don't know. Never been
in it myself."

"I've never seen a gold mine—even an abandoned
one," Ted said. "I think I'll look it over if you don't
mind."

"Sure—why not?" Prospector said. "Won't take
long."

They walked over to the entrance. It was nothing

more than a square hole about ten feet across. It had been cut through the hill, and the sides and roof were supported by huge native timbers. The entrance was littered with rocks. There were a few puddles of water that had trickled there from melting snow. Ted did not consider going back into the mine at that time because he hadn't brought his flashlight along. He was just ready to leave when he happened to look down. There, in one of the silt-covered puddles, was a huge print. He pointed to it and even as he did, the hair on the back of his neck seemed to stand on end.

"Prospector," he said. "What's that?"

"A bear track," Prospector answered. "It looks like you've stumbled onto a den. I said nobody would trap a bear—but now, I'm not so sure. If you use your head, son, I reckon you might surprise Mr. Bruin after all."

9. A BLOW FALLS

AFTER saying good-by to Prospector, Ted jumped into his canoe. He paddled swiftly around the edge of the lake. There were several canoes from camp in the small lake that joined the larger one. What, he wondered, could the campers be doing in there. He turned the canoe and headed for the lake's entrance. He turned in, paddled down a narrow stream for a hundred yards. The stream emptied into the second lake. This lake was no more than a hundred yards across. He noticed now that the canoes were empty, that the campers were all up on the bank. There was considerable shouting and yelling. Ted drove his canoe into the bank, stepped out. He pulled the prow of the canoe up onto the bank so it would not drift. Then he walked ahead to where the crowd had gathered. He was surprised to see Pudge Lawson standing on the outer fringe of the crowd. Pudge saw him coming.

"I wondered how long it would take you to appear

when you found out what was going on," Pudge Lawson exclaimed.

"I still don't know what's going on," Ted said. "What is?"

"Take a look if you want to see something. Rocky Stone was fishing here this afternoon and he hooked into a big rainbow trout. He's been fighting the fish for more than an hour. He is afraid to try to land it because he hasn't a landing net and his line isn't very strong. If he tries to lift the trout out of water, he's afraid the line will snap. So there's nothing to do but play the trout until it gets so tired it gives up."

"From what I hear about rainbows," Ted exclaimed, "they don't give up. You jerk them out of the water and they start fighting all over again. I'd say Rocky has a tough job on his hands."

They moved closer. Despite the fact that Ted was watching a rival, he got a lot of satisfaction from seeing the fight that was taking place. Rocky had indeed hooked a large trout. Once, the fish cleared the water and it appeared to be at least six pounds in weight. It wasn't as large a fish as Brown Beauty, but nevertheless, it was larger than any that had been pulled out.

The trout was running back and forth with the fly. Rocky could only keep the slack out of his line and let the fish play. It was a beautiful sight. The rainbow would race out across the lake and would suddenly leap high into the air and try to throw the hook. Then it would plunge to the depths again and the battle would begin anew. The sun was rapidly disappearing and Ted realized that in the darkness the battle would be much more difficult.

"Say, Rocky, if you had hooked that fish in the big lake, you would be a cinch for the hundred points for fishing." It was Rex Lawrence who spoke. Rex Lawrence was leading the fishing contest. "As it is, though, I'm still safe. You don't know how glad I am that you hooked that beauty where you did."

"Yeah," Rocky muttered. "That's my luck all right. Too bad I couldn't have caught this trout in the big lake . . ." Rocky suddenly stopped dead still. The frown on his face seemed to melt away. In its place came a confident smile. "Say, the rules say that all you have to do is *catch* your fish in the big lake. Well, I'm catching this one there. Just watch me." Rocky turned to one of his cronies, Lem Perkins. "Get in our canoe, Lem. Go ahead, do as I say. When I give you the nod, start paddling toward the big lake."

Lem climbed in and Rocky got in behind him. It was soon evident that Rocky was going to try trickery. What he had in mind was easy enough to see. With Lem paddling, Rocky played the trout from out of the back end of the canoe. If he could keep the trout hooked and drag it from the small lake to the large one, then he could lift it out and say that he had caught it in the big lake. There was logic in what he was doing

—but there didn't seem to be much sportsmanship in it. The others got into their canoes and began to follow. You could hear the grumblings.

"Aw, what if you do catch the fish, Rocky? How can you have the nerve to count it? You know the rules weren't meant to be taken that way. Have a heart. Give the rest of us a chance."

"If they didn't want their rules to be taken this way, then why didn't they make them to cover everything?" Rocky demanded heatedly. "It takes more than luck to win things. You have to use your brains. I'm using mine, see? I'll be catching the fish in the big lake—and I know Jeff Jones will back me up when I take the fish to him."

Ted and Pudge had been following in silence. Ted secretly had hoped the trout would break away. That would immediately put an end to something that might turn into a bad situation. But as Rocky's canoe got closer and closer to the big lake, it became more evident that such would not be the case. The trout was hooked securely and it had been fighting so long that it was wearing out. Feebler and feebler became the trout's tugs. Finally when the canoe emerged into the big lake, the rainbow quit fighting altogether. With a cry of triumph, Rocky leaned over the side of the boat. His hand darted into the water and when it came up, he had the trout hooked through the gills with his fingers. The trout barely wriggled. Rocky held the prize up so that all could see.

"I guess this is the end of the fishing contest," he gloated. "If this baby weighs a pound, he weighs at least six and a half. You, Ted Moran. Why don't you smile about it, huh? I'd think you'd like it. It gives you something to shoot at."

"Do you want me to let him have it with a paddle?" Pudge asked in a low, tense voice. "You just say the word."

"There are more ways than one to do a job right," Ted said softly. "Let him crow. When the time comes, he'll wish he'd kept quiet. It's hard to take back something, once it's said."

"Now look here, Ted Moran. You're talking through your hat. You'd like to beat him, sure. Who wouldn't? But you know and I know that you can't. There's only one fish in this neck of the woods that would compare with that one—and nobody's going to catch Brown Beauty. Be sensible."

"Maybe not," Ted admitted. "But we've got another two months to wait. A lot can happen in that length of time. And you can be sure of one thing—little Teddy isn't quitting just because the future looks dark. See if I do."

"There's one thing about it," Pudge admitted. "When Jeff Jones hears how the fish was caught, he

might rule that it won't count. We can at least hope
that will happen, can't we?"

"We can hope," Ted said. "But I don't know if it
will work."

Ted was right. That night, Jeff Jones listened to the
story of how the fish was caught. "To be perfectly
frank," he said, "we made the rule so that none of you
would wander off into the canyons in search of other
lakes. It never occurred to any of us that such a thing
as this could happen."

"But according to the rules," Rocky said, "I should
get the points. The rules say that any trout taken out
of the big lake is to be counted in the fishing contest.
Well, I have proof that I took mine out of there. I've
already told you that."

"Very well—I see that you are going to hold out for
a strict interpretation of the rules. There is nothing
more that I can say. Your fish weighs six pounds and
three ounces. I'll list you on the board along with the
others."

Ted and Pudge started for their cabin. "Doesn't
that tie you, though," Pudge exclaimed heatedly.
"There goes another hundred points. I tell you that
guy is beginning to get in my hair. If I'm not careful,
I'll be parting his hair with a canoe paddle. But you're
not giving up, Ted. I won't let you. You'll have plenty
of chances to get even with him."

On their way to the cabin they passed the bulletin
board.

The fire of competition was burning brightly within Ted. He studied the standings on the board awhile, then said to Jeff Jones, "When does the trapping contest close?"

"Let's see—it's July the first. There won't be any more snow down here until fall. We haven't done much with trapping and the time is getting late. I think we'd better put a date limit for trapping at about July 15th. Any of you fellows who want to trap can talk it over with Indian Jim. He's an expert. Decide what you'd like to catch and he'll give you some pointers."

Ted nudged Pudge. "Come with me," he said quietly. "We're going to visit Indian Jim." A few moments later they found him. "Indian Jim," Ted said, "how about getting some trapping information from you?"

The Indian invited them into a small work shed. He turned on a light. The room contained all sorts of miscellaneous articles, such as extra tennis rackets, fishing poles and such. Jim said, "What animal Ted want to trap? Wolf be nice."

Jim had taken down a trap. It was a long piece of metal, split half down the middle. Jim pulled the two pieces of metal apart, placing a spring between them. "This wolf trap," he said. "Wolf step on spring. Steel catch wolf by foot and hold till trapper come catch him."

Ted said, "That's all right, Jim. But what I'm interested in is a big trap. Something three or four times that large. You see, I'm going after a bear. Have you got a bear trap?"

The red man arched his sparse eyebrows. "Tenderfeet ask for much trouble. Bear hard to trap. Dangerous, too."

But Ted had an idea. He could not get the thought of that bear print out of his mind. So he told Jim his story. He said that he was going to set his trap at night when the bear was out of the mine shaft. Then he would leave and wait until the bear returned to the cave. After that he thought he could hear the bear growling if it got caught.

"Plan sound good," Jim said thoughtfully. "But be careful. Don't get caught in mine if bear return. Tenderfeet would make heap lot of bear food."

"Yeah . . ." Ted muttered. "I thought of that, too. But that's the part I don't want to think about. Well, give me the trap. I haven't too much time left and I can't waste any of it."

Pudge wiped the perspiration from his forehead, "This is one time," he muttered, "when I'm glad you're leaving me out of your plans. Br-rrr! I wouldn't be in your boots for anything."

"Aw, I haven't anything to worry about," Ted said. But even as he said it, Fate was getting ready to look in on the scene. And this time Fate was mixing up a strange potion indeed. . . .

10. TOMB OF DOOM

For three days Ted Moran was up before daylight. He would row across the lake, beach his boat and then climb the hill to the old abandoned mine shaft. His purpose, of course, was to watch for Mr. Bruin to see what time he usually returned home from his night forays. But not once did he see the bear.

And then something happened that caused Ted to change all of his plans. One evening he came in from the lake. The moment he saw Pudge's scowl, he knew that something was wrong.

"You'll step on your lower lip if you're not careful," Ted said. "Get it off your chest. What's happened today?"

"Plenty—and it's all bad. Come on. I'll show you."

Puzzled, Ted followed Pudge. They walked across the clearing to the small cabin that housed Rocky Stone. Rocky was outside and there was a large crowd around him. The moment Ted saw Rocky, he had a hint of what it was all about. Lying on the ground in front of Rocky was a wolf. A huge fellow. And still clinging to the wolf's foot was a steel trap.

"For three weeks," Rocky said importantly, "I've been trying to catch this fellow. This afternoon when I went to look at my trap I found him. This may not win first place for me in the trapping contest—but I notice none of you other guys have caught anything but chipmunks. Looks to me like the gold star is a cinch."

Ted poked Pudge. "Come on," he whispered hoarsely, "let's get out of here. I don't like so much hot air on a warm night."

The inseparable pals walked over to their own cabin. When they got inside, Ted first made sure that they were alone. Then he began to change clothes. He put on a heavy wool shirt. He put on leather boots and as an afterthought, picked up his hunting knife. Then taking his flashlight, he looked quickly around the room to see if he had left anything.

"Say, where are you going with that tough look on your face?" Pudge demanded. "Don't tell me you're not going to be here tonight. You know how tough they are when you stay out after hours."

"They're tough, all right," Ted said. "And they have a right to be. A tenderfoot hasn't any business running around in the woods alone at night—unless he knows exactly where he is going and what he's going to do when he gets there. Come on, Pudge. I'm going to let you paddle me across the lake."

Ted picked up the large steel bear trap and then Pudge got the idea. "Wait a minute—you're not going trapping are you? Why—you couldn't get me to go out alone at night if my life depended on it. What if you meet a bear? You know that you can't club them to death the way you did the wolf. Sometimes I think you're crazy, Ted."

Pudge continued to try to dissuade Ted as they moved across the lake in the canoe.

"Quit worrying, Pudge—say, do you notice anything?"

Pudge looked around. "No . . . not unless you mean the weather? I hadn't noticed that heavy bank of clouds before. And it's lightning over there beyond the peaks, too. That settles it. You can't go out on a night like this. Suppose a bad storm comes up. What then?"

"I've been drenched before," Ted said. "I'm not afraid of rain. Come to think of it, I do think it's going to rain. When we first came out the wind was in the north. Now it has shifted around and I can smell moisture in the air. Funny how fast a storm comes up in the mountains. One minute the moon is out and the next there's a bank of clouds rolling in. Wait a minute —keep this boat headed for the shore. I'm not turning around. No siree. Not after going to all of this fuss."

Pudge continued to propel the craft along in silence. It wasn't until they reached Prospector's dock that Pudge said, "Well, if you're going to be stubborn and go anyway, do at least one thing for me. Tell me exactly when you expect to be home. If anything should happen to you and you aren't back to camp by that time, then I'll know I ought to send out a searching party for you."

"Okay, okay," Ted said. "I'm going to wait for the bear to leave. He didn't leave all afternoon—I watched. I have the idea that there's one bear that doesn't start out until late at night. I'll do this: When the bear leaves, I'll wait a few minutes. Then I'll go inside the cave and set the trap. After that, I'll come out again and wait for the bear to return to the mine shaft. In any event, I won't be over here any later than daylight. If I'm not home by then," Ted grinned, "you can come after me. But whatever you do, don't come before."

Ted took his rifle, slung it under his arm, waved a silent good-by to Pudge, then started up the hill. He noticed that the wind had increased as he walked silently up the grade. The lightning flashes were more pronounced and this time there was no doubt that the rain was on the way.

Ted reached the top of the hill, took his place about fifty yards away from the entrance of the mine. The mine tunnel looked as black as pitch and Ted shuddered at the thought of what mysteries the cavern might contain. He lay there, peering from behind a small evergreen. He felt a splash of rain on the back of his right hand. Then another. . . .

Suddenly he saw something that thrilled him to the core, and at the same time made his blood run cold. A huge black shape had lumbered from the mouth of the mine. It was a bear. . . . . the largest bear Ted had ever seen. The bear stood there, sniffing suspiciously. Ted was thankful that he was downwind so that it was impossible for the animal to get his scent. He lay there, scarcely daring to breathe. Every muscle was tense. Bruin, after casting a curious, sidelong glance in Ted's direction, suddenly began to lumber the other way. He went over the hill and out of sight.

The rain began to slap against the ground and soon there were small puddles. Suddenly the lightning crashed loudly and the heavens poured forth a veritable flood of water. Ted decided Bruin was far enough away from him to make entering the mine safe. So he advanced swiftly. The moment he came to the entrance he turned on his flash beam. The light cut a path through the gloom. Ted stepped in out of the rain. Carefully he flashed the light ahead of him. He walked forward about ten paces. Here the tunnel took a sharp turn to the right. It narrowed considerably. There were broken-down timbers that had once kept the

roof from caving in. Now they were half-rotted through
and strewn over the passage way. It was now necessary
for Ted to stoop low to go deeper into the cavern.

The twists and turns grew closer together. Cobwebs
brushed his cheeks, hung stickily against his skin. At
last after several minutes of walking, he came to a narrow passage tunnelled out of solid granite. Emerging
on the other side he discovered that he was in a rather
large room. He flashed his light around quickly. The
room looked to be ten feet square and was about ten
feet high. There was a ledge about seven feet up on
one wall. It looked large enough to support a bear.
There were scratches on the walls of the room and Ted
decided that the bear stayed up on the ledge.

Ted set to work immediately. He set the bear trap.
It was a large piece of steel with jaws that were rugged
and as sharp as razors. The trap was so strong that it
took all of Ted's weight upon the spring to get the
thing apart. Then when Ted had it ready to spring,
he placed it on the floor of the room. He knew that
when the bear came lumbering in he would catch one
of his huge paws in the trap. There was a strong chain
extending from the trap and this Ted tied securely to
one of the timbers that looked strong enough to hold it.

It was at that instant that he heard the noise. First
it came to him so gently that he hardly paid any attention to it. It was more like a breath of wind, a faint,
fluttering rustle. But when he heard it again, he knew

that it wasn't his imagination playing tricks on him. Suddenly his hair began to prickle at the ends. He felt goose flesh break out all over him.

The noise sounded like the scraping of bristles across rock. Ted's heart was now in his throat. Had he been careless? Had he allowed himself to be trapped? For the rustling sound seemed to come from behind him.

The sound grew louder. And then came the first clue to what it was. It was a growl. A snarl. But it was certainly not the growl of a large bear. It was too high-pitched to be that. Ted shone his flashlight around, then on an impulse, he flashed the light up to the ledge of rock that extended from one of the walls. What he saw was a great relief. Two furry noses were sticking over the ledge. There were two tiny bear cubs and both of them were more bewildered than they were afraid. Almost immediately Ted forgot the purpose of his mission.

Ted stood up. "Hello there, little fellows," he said. "Come on down here, let me play with you. I'm not going to hurt you."

But the cubs weren't so sure about it. When Ted reached for one of them, he scampered back away from the ledge and let out a sharp growl of fear. So keeping the light shining above him, Ted climbed up the ledge.

He stood there a moment, eyeing the cubs. He had never seen animals that looked so cunning. They were like big, woolly dogs. He wanted to pick one of them up and play with him. He extended a finger gingerly. One of the cubs, braver than the other, growled as loudly as it could.

"Now see here, little fellow," Ted soothed, "you know I'm not going to harm you. Here, let me prove it to you."

Ted leaned over, picked the cuddly animal up in his arms. The bear cub let out a startled yip, then began to fight furiously. But Ted held on and soon the cub was subdued. It even became quite playful. The other cub, evidently still frightened, let out a fearful growl for an animal his size. Ted was just ready to reach down and pick up the other one when his heart froze in his throat.

The roar in his ears was like the blast of a cannon. This time there was no doubt about it. The old bear was coming home. The mother bear. Ted knew that he was doomed. He had heard stories of how a mother animal would fight until the death for its young.

The mother bear's growl rang out again. This time so close that Ted could almost hear the footpads of the huge animal. He knew that he could not jump down and get his gun. He had foolishly left it lying on the floor of the cave. . . .

Now he heard the bear plunge into the entrance of the passage that was just outside the large room. Ted thought, "Oh, Pudge, if I had only listened to you."

And then he had time to think no more because things happened too fast after that.

Old mother bear's angry nose came charging through the entrance. Big black eyes flashed against the beam of the flashlight. Long fangs were bared. A gruff, dangerous roar came up from the bear's throat. The bear, seeing the light up where her babies had been, now increased the fury of her charge. She reared up on hind legs. And then it happened.

One foot hit the lever of the trap. The huge animal let out a roar of rage and pain. It leaped high, tried to jump out of the steel thing that held it by the hind leg. The trap was chained to one of the timbers and as the bear leaped at Ted, the timber shook. Ted could feel the bear's hot breath against him. He kept the light blazing in the animal's eyes, hoping, praying that something would happen to save him. He was in the tightest spot of his life. What could he do? Where could he turn? Already the bear seemed to be loosening the timber. Each leap carried it closer and closer to Ted. Ted was cringing back against the rear wall. The claws came closer, closer. Now they were but inches from him. The chain clanged at every leap. Each growl of the bear seemed to be the death cry that was to seal Ted's doom. He had now given up hope. It was but a moment or two away, a few more jerks on the chain—then the bear would be loose.

Ted watched, fascinated, as the furry black animal gathered itself for another leap. Legs that were stronger than new steel were now bunched up, coiled. Then came the spring. And with that spring came pandemonium. For the chain that had been attached to the wooden timber had held—and the timber was jerked loose from the wall. The ceiling came crashing down. There was a momentary rumble of noise, then the room was filled with dust. The mother bear was growling furiously, but it was so dusty that Ted could not see. He turned his flashlight off, saving the battery. He had no idea how badly the room had been damaged, or how badly the bear was hurt, if, indeed, that proved to be the case. He waited for perhaps ten minutes. By then he felt the dust should have settled. This time he turned the light down to where the entrance had been. And it gave him another rude shock. The timber had let the ceiling rocks come crashing down. A rockslide had started and now the tiny entrance was buried under tons and tons of rock. Ted Moran was entombed! But worse than that, he was entombed in a pit with an angry old mother bear.

Gingerly he turned the beam of light in the bear's direction. The old bear was entangled in the fallen timbers. She fought at them but gradually, unable to free herself, she lessened her efforts. But Ted knew that soon, once she rested, the struggle to free herself would begin over again.

Ted turned the light around over the floor. He saw something else that puzzled him. Where the floor of the cave had been dry when he entered it, there was now about an inch of water on it. He decided the rain was seeping down the tunnel.

He waited for what seemed hours. Actually it probably wasn't more than one hour. During that time the old mother bear had renewed her struggling and because Ted would rather have met his fate in the dark, he had kept the light out.

But now he turned it on again—and to his surprise, the water was almost a foot deep. The mother bear, too, seemed puzzled over it. Puzzled, and a little afraid. The bear began to growl again, but there was a sort of whine in the growl that had not been there before. Ted understood at once. The animal, seeing the water creep up, was afraid of drowning. Before long, the water would be up above the bear's nose—unless the animal could be freed from the mass of fallen timbers.

"Poor fellow," Ted thought. It did not occur to him at the moment that the same fate awaited him as the one the bear was looking forward to. Where at first he had thought his life would end under the charge of the mother bear, he gradually began to understand that he and the old bear had a common thing to fear. The water was slowly rising higher.

Were they to be drowned like rats in a trap? It looked that way. Ted did not have a watch but he knew that it couldn't yet be midnight and he couldn't possibly expect to have help before morning! Morning—how far away that seemed now. By morning the watery tomb would long ago have been filled. The bear was threshing about wildly now. Again Ted turned the light down below and what he saw caused his heart to wring with pity. The water was up over the bear's back. The animal was turning fear filled eyes up toward Ted. There were no growls of anger now—only growls of fear.

Suddenly Ted made up his mind. "Lady," he said grimly, "I know how you must feel. And even though I did come in here to get you, I've changed my mind. I'm taking a chance with you. Just don't get scared of me. . . ."

Ted eased down off his perch. The water was up almost to his armpits. The bear glared at him. There was a growl or two, but then they subsided. The old animal seemed to realize that Ted was not there to harm her—that they were two individuals caught in the same dire predicament. Ted inched closer. Flashing the light around, he saw what was wrong. Two timbers had fallen crossways and the one to which the bear was chained was underneath. Ted lifted the top one and that let the other go free. Immediately the wooden timber began to float. Ted scurried back upon his perch before the animal could discover that it was free and perhaps slap at him with one of those huge,

death-dealing paws. He was not a moment too soon.
The bear, discovering that it could now move about,
reared up on its hind legs and began to growl again.
The animal, by stretching, could reach the front edge
of the ledge upon which Ted was sitting. Ted shoved
the two cubs out in front of him. The mother bear began to lick the cubs as the frightened babies nuzzled
up to her.

That seemed to satisfy her for awhile. The water
was now almost up to the top of the ledge. In a minute
or two it would cover the ledge and Ted would be
sitting in the water. The ceiling was only about three
feet above the ledge. Ted could not stand up on it.

The water slowly crept higher, higher. It certainly
must have been a cloudburst, Ted decided. It would
take millions of gallons of water to flood that mine. . . .

The water was now up to the bear's face. The huge
animal gave a lunge—and then she was sitting on the
ledge beside Ted. As for Ted, he was too petrified to
move a muscle. He just sat there, not saying a word,
scarcely breathing. But gradually, as the water closed
in on them, he lost his timidity. He turned on the light
again. The mother bear blinked. But she made no
move toward Ted. It was almost as if she realized the
predicament they faced together.

Ted said, "I'm sorry, old girl. I got us into this mess."

Ted reached out, touched one of the cubs. The little
animal snuggled closer to his wet knee. He realized

that he could comfort the cubs. He lifted them under his arms, let them rest upon his knees. That kept them higher off the ledge and gave them a chance to breathe without sucking in water. Now, the water was nearly up to Ted's shoulders. He held the cubs up close to him so that their noses were pressing against the ceiling. The mother bear would look at Ted, then at her cubs. She seemed to understand that Ted was doing everything possible. Ted kept his flashlight dry on a rock above his head.

The lap, lap, lap of the water in the death chamber was dismal in his ears. How could it rain as much as this? How could so much water flow into one room?

Suddenly Ted let out a startled shout. The bears blinked at him. "Wait a minute," he exclaimed, "I've got it. This water can't be coming in from the entrance, because we're higher than the entrance. It has to be coming in from up above us and if it is, there's an entrance above us."

He swung the light above him. The ceiling was weirdly illuminated. He flung the beam around him —and then he found it. The water was gushing in from a crack in the ceiling. Ted tried to reason that out. What could it be? The water couldn't be rolling off the top of the hill and down through a crack. No, that water had to be stored some place. But where? Somewhere above was another mine passage. Water had stored in there and when the entrance caved in, the crack had appeared. Then the water had seeped down into the tunnel below. Somewhere up above was a water-filled room—and beyond that lay freedom. But how to break through to that other tunnel? Ted had no way of knowing how far through rock it was.

It might be two inches, and again it might be two feet. But regardless of how far it was, Ted would have to open it fast, or it would be too late. Suddenly, he got an inspiration. The bear's chain was still hanging to the timber and the timber was bobbing around close to Ted's face. He knew that minutes were short. So he dropped the flashlight to the water-covered ledge. Then using both hands, he placed the bear cubs up close to their mother. They clung to her, lifting their noses out of the water. Ted reached out, grasped the floating timber. It was heavy, but the water helped to hold it and make it lighter. Ted backed up to the edge of the ledge until he was standing about three feet from where the water was flowing in the crack.

He pulled the timber back, aiming the end of it at the crack. Then using every atom of muscle in his young body, he shoved the timber at the place in the wall where the water was gushing in. The timber shivered as it crashed against the rock—and then it broke through. Water came gushing through the larger hole, tearing mud and rock with it. The next thing Ted knew he was being propelled upward. He had broken through to the water-filled cavern above him and he was now shooting to the surface. He felt himself come out of the water. He opened his eyes, took a deep breath. He was in a dark cavern of some sort and was in water up to his neck. Feeling up above him, he touched something hard—a rock ceiling. He stayed there, treading water, wondering what to do next. His feet touched something solid. He stepped up onto it, rested. That was when he remembered the waterproof packet in his pocket—a packet that contained matches. He groped for them, struck one of them against the ceiling. Now in the glow, he could see where he was. He was indeed in a mine shaft. He could see steps leading upward to the left of him. The bear cubs were scampering up it and the mother bear was trying to follow but the trap and timber made it difficult. Ted lifted the timber, carried it. The old mother bear hobbled along ahead of him, seemingly grateful for the favor.

Eventually they came to a shaft of light. Ted realized that it was daylight and somehow that cheered him. They stepped out into the daylight, found themselves on the top of the ground. There was a shout from the left, "There he is—oh, Ted. Ted Moran."

Ted turned, saw half the camp headed toward him. He saw Pudge in the lead. The mother bear growled and jerked at the timber. Ted, understanding, shouted, "Stay where you are, every one of you. Say, is Jeff Jones in the crowd?"

"Here I am, Ted. What do you want?"

"Do you see this trap on the bear's foot? Well, the rules say that the person who traps the largest animal wins. It doesn't specify that the animal has to be brought in dead. Maybe I'm funny, but this old bear and I have gone through a lot together. I'm letting her loose. I get my hundred points, don't I?"

The camp director, after recovering from his astonishment, said, "I'm certain you will be entitled to them." As for Ted, he reached down, unsprung the old mother's foot from the trap. He saw that she was not badly hurt. The cubs were frolicking in the sunlight and the old mother, giving one backward glance at Ted, lumbered away with them. Ted Moran had never felt more pleased with himself in his entire life.

11. PROSPECTOR GETS SICK

TED's experience with the bear was the talk of camp for the next few days. Rocky redoubled his trapping efforts, but at the end of the contest, the most he could add to his collection was a chipmunk that had stumbled into a wolf trap. So the scores went up and for the first time, Ted was leading.

Ted Moran: 200   Rocky Stone: 180

It was late afternoon when the scores were posted. Most of the campers were gathered around the bulletin board. Many of them congratulated Ted for he had proved himself to be a good sport as well as a fiery competitor.

Jeff Jones came up to Ted and asked him to step into his office a moment. Pudge nudged Ted. "There it is. I told you it was coming. I knew you wouldn't get off as easy as it looked. Well, I'll keep my fingers crossed. If you need any help, I'll come at your yell. I only hope Jones goes easy on you."

135

Ted grunted. He had wondered how long he could go before Jeff Jones said something about his nocturnal adventure. Would he be expelled from camp? What would happen to him?

Once inside the camp director's office, there was little time wasted. Jeff Jones said, "Ted, what time did you leave camp to go on that trapping expedition? Tell the truth, now."

"You needn't worry about my telling the truth," Ted said quietly. "I left the evening before and I was gone all night."

"So you deliberately broke a camp rule. Why, Ted?"

"Well," Ted said thoughtfully, "I didn't look at it that way. You see, sir, winning this medal for being the best camper means a lot to me. When Rocky caught that wolf—well, I just knew that I had to get something larger. I wanted a bear. I knew, sir, where this bear lived and I also knew that the job would have to be done at night. Then, too, I didn't want anyone reminding me of it if I failed in my attempt. So I made my plans and did the thing I thought best."

The camp director sat there, tapping his foot against the floor, wrinkling his brow thoughtfully, Finally he looked up at Ted.

"Yes . . . yes, I can see your point all right. And there is one thing in your favor—before you left, you told Pudge where you were going and what you were going to do. This may seem rather odd to you—you broke a rule and should be punished. But, well, young man, I would have done exactly the same thing if I had been you. Rules are flexible things. Here we try to teach you to be self-reliant. We don't want to make it hard on anyone."

"Well . . . thank you, sir. It's nice of you to take it this way. I thought I was doing right, but I couldn't be sure how you would take it. I'm relieved, to say the least."

Ted got up to leave, but the camp director motioned that the interview was not yet over. Puzzled, Ted remained seated.

"I'm not punishing you for what you did, Ted. But there is one thing that we have both overlooked. The rifle. You lost it and it belonged to the camp. It wasn't an expensive article, but for that matter, it wasn't yours to lose, either. So I must insist that you pay for it. No, I'm not asking for actual money. Instead I am going to let you work it out. For the next week you will get up an hour early and help out in the kitchen."

Ted sighed inwardly at the thought of having to roll out at five—he realized, however, that this was an easy way out of the whole affair. He had earned his points in trapping and he was willing to suffer almost any kind of punishment in order to get to keep them.

In a way the punishment didn't turn out so badly.

For it gave Ted an opportunity to make an acquaint-ance that was to prove valuable to him later. The man was the Chinese cook, Charlie.

Charlie was a small, roly-poly Chinese. When Ted reported to him early the next morning, Charlie threw his hands up in mock anger but immediately put Ted to work and kept him busy until after breakfast. He was the last one to take off his apron and hang up his towel. He started to leave but Charlie stopped him.

"I like you. You make work easier for me."

Ted grinned, clapped the small chunky Chinese on the shoulder. "See you tomorrow morning, Charlie," he said. "Right now I've got some fishing to do. I'm after a certain trout that doesn't seem to want to be hooked. So long, Charlie."

Ted returned to his cabin. He found Pudge waiting. Pudge looked up suspiciously. "I've been worried about you, fellow. Say, was it tough? I saw we had po-tatoes for breakfast. Bet you had to peel 'em, huh? Tell me all about it. I'm busting."

"There's nothing much to tell," Ted said. "I did have to peel the potatoes. But I didn't mind that so much and. . ."

"Say," Pudge interrupted. "Are you crazy? Who ever heard of anyone not minding peeling potatoes? What else did you do?"

"Oh, nothing much—helped with the dishes and a few things like that. But it was fun, really. And the fellow I work for, he's okay. A goodhearted Chinese—you've seen him around. But I haven't time to stand around and talk about it. Right now I'm digging out my fishing tackle. I'm going after Brown Beauty."

Pudge sat down on the edge of his bunk. "On a hot day like this? I'd rather pack a lunch and go out into the forest for a lazy afternoon of doing nothing. Besides, why be in such a hurry to catch that fish? You're ahead in the gold star contest."

"I'm ahead right now," Ted said. "But stop to consider this angle. If the contest was to close right now—on the fishing, I mean—Rocky would get first and Rex Lawrence would get second. I wouldn't even be in it. No, I can't afford to wait. I have to get at least second. So I'm headed for the lake again."

"Need I remind you, my impulsive young friend, that there are other things besides fishing?"

"Good-by, my fat friend," Ted said. "I can see where you want to spend the afternoon by yourself and it's all the same with me. I'll see you some time later. If I get interested, I may not be in for lunch. I'll stick an orange or two in my pocket."

Ted left immediately. He was wearing rubber fishing boots over a pair of old trousers. He was stripped to the waist and the July sun was blazing down upon his muscular young body, turning it a deep, golden bronze. Here it was the middle of July. By the end of August the summer season in the mountains would be

gone. While the rest of the country was getting ready
for a beautiful autumn, early winter would come to
the mountains. Now as Ted walked toward the lake, it
was hard to realize that such a short time remained.

Ted found an idle canoe. Indian Jim was sitting on
a rock close by. The Indian gave a friendly greeting as
he saw Ted.

"Hi, Indian Jim," he said. "Going fishing today?"

"No. Jim got work to do. But tenderfeet catch trout
today. Lots of trout. Indian Jim read signs. Fish want
big yellow fly today. See if Jim not right."

"Thanks for the tip," Ted said. "I'll try a yellow fly
the first thing."

Ted put on a fly called a yellow bee. It was nothing
more than a small yellow hook about an inch long.
The length of the hook was wrapped with yellow yarn
so that the hook could not be seen. Next two long yellow fingers dangled from the hook, like wings. These
yellow fingers were nothing but dyed feathers. When
the fly hit the water, it looked like an injured insect,
unable to get up off the water.

Three quarters of the way across the lake, Ted
stopped, let the craft begin to drift. He let out about
twenty feet of line and slowly began to cast. Once,
twice, three times he whipped the line out across the
boat's prow. Each time he would slowly reel the line in
so that the fly moved easily across the surface of the
water.

The third time he began to draw the fly in and that was when it happened. A rainbow trout, about sixteen inches long, leaped high out of the water. Ted gave his line a light jerk and the hook was set tightly in the trout's mouth. The fun began. The shimmering rainbow dived into the water, began to slash back and forth at the end of the line. Ted kept the slack out, let the rainbow play. But the fish was not giving up.

Suddenly it turned and came back toward the boat. Ted took a paddle, jerked it around so that the boat swung out of the way. The line passed across the bow of the boat. Ted, reeling in swiftly, took up most of the line. He began to apply the pressure now. Gradually the rainbow weakened and after a ten-minute fight, Ted leaned over the side of the boat and pulled in his prize. The rainbow was his first catch of the day. Now thoroughly confident that his yellow fly was the one to use, he paddled over to the north edge of the lake and began to work in and out among the rocks. Within two hours he had caught half a dozen nice trout. As he caught the last one, he looked up and was rather surprised to see that he was close to the dock of Prospector's cabin. Ted glanced toward the cabin. He saw that no smoke was coming out of the chimney.

"Hello, there, Prospector," Ted called. "Are you here?"

Ted stood there in his boat, listening. He heard nothing. Puzzled, he got up, walked up the path to the shack. He saw the shovel and pick, leaning in a small excavation. Surely the old man would not leave his tools behind him if he really had gone. Ted went up to the door. It was half open.

"Prospector—are you here? It's me . . . Ted Moran."

He heard a low groan. Inside he found the old man lying on his bunk. The old man's eyes were bright and his cheeks, beneath the thin gray beard, were flushed.

"You're sick, old fellow," Ted said. "What's wrong?"

The old man smiled. "I . . . I stumbled while I was digging the other day. I must have hit my head on a rock. Anyway, I got myself knocked out. It musta rained—because when I woke up, it was night and I was layin' in water. Come near drownin'. I musta got chilled too much. Ain't been worth anything since. Glad you come, fellow."

"What you need," Ted said, "is some hot food. Wait a minute. I've got some fish in my canoe. I'll get them and we'll have ourselves a feed. Where's your ax? I'll step outside and chop some fire wood."

"I . . . I have food, Ted. I . . . I reckon I needn't eat yours."

Ted said, "You save your food. We'll eat these fish. Do you want them to spoil?"

Ted went outside, found the ax. He found several half-dead evergreens nearby and after a few moments he had cut them down. He took some of the dried foliage, cut up an armload of sticks and then carried them inside. In a moment he had a hot fire started. Ted went down to the lake. He had a hunting knife in his fishing kit and it didn't take long to dress the trout. When he returned to the cabin, he put the fish in the heavy iron oven, placed a small amount of water over them and let them bake. He found a tin of coffee and put this on to boil.

Ted opened the windows so that there could be plenty of fresh air and sunshine. Finally he had the meal finished. There was plenty of fish and a thin, tasty broth. They drank their coffee without sugar or cream. Ted had tasted much better, but Prospector smacked his lips appreciatively. "Best meal I ever tasted," he said. "Makes me feel like a new man."

"What you need," Ted said, "is plenty of sleep, now that you've eaten. I'll get you some fresh water from the spring. You go ahead and go to sleep. I have to get back to camp, but I'll be back real soon."

"You . . . you needn't bother about me, young feller."

"I'm the doctor," Ted said. "You'd better do as I say. Get to sleep now. I'll see you later."

Ted fished back across the lake. When he came in, it was almost time for supper. He took his fish into the kitchen, gave them to Charlie. Charlie, who liked fish better than anything else, was pleased. But Ted said, "I want a return favor, Charlie. I know a fellow who is sick. Tonight I'm going to visit him. Will you give me some kind of food that will make him well?"

"Man sick? Sure, I'll fix him. Come back after supper."

And that night Ted did. After dark, he got a small bucket of steaming soup from the goodhearted Chinese. There were also a few cans of milk and vegetables.

12. A LESSON IN WOODCRAFT

TED continued to visit Prospector. The old man responded to Ted's careful nursing. Ted chopped his wood, carried him newspapers and magazines that had been discarded in camp. He was getting nothing out of it but the satisfaction of knowing that it was a job well done. Of course, he was careful not to let anyone but Pudge in on his secret.

Because of the Prospector and the amount of care he required, Ted neglected his own chances to win the gold star award. Days when he might have been fishing, he would be up by the old Prospector's camp, chopping wood for the firebox or doing some of the many things that were necessary for his comfort.

During the last week in July they had an all-day sports carnival with Redskin Camp which was similar to All-American Camp. There was a baseball game in the morning and a water carnival in the afternoon. Since Ted had been tending to Old Prospector, he participated in the gala events of the day without having practiced as much as he should have. At the end of the day the standings on the board were:

Rocky: 260   Ted: 230

As July faded into August, the campers became aware of the fact that there was but one month left. One month, and so many things yet to be done. One morning the campers were ordered to dress in their heaviest clothes and to bring their bed rolls and their small cooking outfits that consisted of a skillet, a dish and knife, fork, and spoon.

"What do you make of it, Ted?" Pudge asked, as they got into their heavy woolens. "Where are we headed now?"

"It's for an outing of some kind," Ted said. "I've heard rumors that we were to have a real hike before going home. This must be it. You know I'm kind of glad about it. I've wanted to get out away from camp and pit myself against nature."

When Ted and Pudge left the cabin, they were well weighted down. Their bed rolls included their cooking utensils and their tents. On their belts they carried hatchets and hunting knives. They walked over to the Administration Building where they found the other campers, similarly attired. The camp director was talking.

"Today," Jeff Jones said, "I'm going to break the news you've long been wondering about. Ever since

we've been in camp we have been learning things about
the woods. Indian Jim has shown you boys how to
mark a trail. He has taught you things about the forest
and about the mountains. You should be able to spend
a few days in the wilderness. Yes, I meant what I said.
I see your startled looks. But you shouldn't feel as you
do—for after all, it has been the purpose of this camp
to teach you how to get along with nature.

"You have wondered how we were going to award
the woodcraft points. Well, you can relax about the
whole matter now. This trip we're taking will be in
the nature of a contest. Each of you fellows pick a
partner. The two of you will be taken far up the mountains by horseback. From the start, you must mark trail
to the best of your abilities. For when you reach the
destination for which you are headed, you will be
turned loose. Your horses will be brought back by the
guides who accompany you. Understand now—each
pair of trail breakers will be taken to a different spot
in the mountains. But all of you will be about equally
distant from camp. It will take all day to ride to where
you are going. Sleep there tonight. Then tomorrow
morning, as early as you can see, start back. The first
pair of men to return to camp will be given one hundred points each for woodcraft. The second pair will
receive second points and so on.

"Some of the fellows have been secretly trained as
guides. They know where each set of fellows is sup-

posed to start from. The guides are ready now. They have horses of their own. The men who are going to make the trip will ride two on a horse. Are there any questions?"

Pudge thought of one. "Suppose," he said, "someone gets lost? Then what? How will that person get back to camp?"

"Your guides will provide you with flares," the camp director said. "In addition, you will be given rifles. One rifle to two men. Those are for your protection. But in case you should happen to get lost, fire your rifle. If you hear no reply to three quick shots, that will mean that you are not close enough to anyone. But don't worry. Wait until night comes. Then shoot your flares off. They will be seen by someone and rescue can be sent out. Well, that's about all there is to tell you. You're going on a great adventure. May the best woodsmen win."

Ted and Pudge climbed up onto the back of a sturdy pony. They were well loaded down. Riding in front of them was a young guide. They started in a westerly direction. First they followed a well-defined path, keeping close to the south shore of the lake. Looking back, Ted could see that other pairs were starting up also. He was relieved to see that Lem and Rocky were going toward the south.

Ted forgot everything but the trip at hand. They

reached a canyon on the south end of the lake and the guide turned up into it. The canyon was covered with rocky boulders and it was also well-forested with huge, fragrantly scented cedars. Because it was necessary for only one of them to mark trail, Ted got off and began to carve little marks in the trees. He made the marks about a hundred steps apart. Some of the time he used rock markings. When small saplings were convenient, Ted would cut through them, pointing out the way.

They went to the top of the canyon, down the other side. They could look in all directions and see nothing but trees, hills and an occasional small stream. After Ted had walked awhile, he got back up on the horse and Pudge took his turn. When Pudge seemed puzzled, he would offer a suggestion as to how to best mark a clear trail. If ever a person wanted to win an event— this was it. Ted had to score that 100 points in woodcraft. Had to! For the day before he had received a letter from his dad. Ted could close his eyes and recall every word of the short letter.

"Dear Ted," his dad had written. "I hear from Pudge's mother that you are doing quite nobly by yourself in the race to become Gold Star Camper. I told you that you could do it. I also hear that you've been having a bit of difficulty with your competitor from State. Don't let it bother you, boy. There is an old saying that cheaters never win. That will hold true in your case. Just keep your chin up and fight with the old Moran spirit.

"There's one thing that I've been holding as a secret. Now I'm going to tell it to you. Your camp closes the first of September. I have been working rather hard this summer and I have decided that I owe myself a vacation. Since I'm anxious to see you, I have decided to run up into the mountains. I will be there for the closing session of camp.

"Perhaps I will be able to see some of the final events of your program. I would like nothing better than to see you win something, Ted. But I shall have my wish. For I will be there when the Gold Star Camper award is made and I already know that you will come through. I hope that you are as pleased about this as I am. I look forward to seeing you, son.

Affectionately, your Dad."

Ted hadn't had the courage to write his father, explaining to him that he was far from winning the award. It was nice having your parent feel such trust and faith in you . . . but sometimes it could be a bit annoying, just as it was proving to be now.

"I simply mustn't think about it," Ted told himself savagely. "I'm in this thing and I've got to do my best to get out of it on the winning side. There's plenty of time for worry later on."

When Pudge began to pant from the exertion of walking, Ted got off and again began to mark trail.

They had come to a very steep cliff, one so rugged that even the horses, with their longer legs, found difficult to climb. It was covered with heavy boulders. There were fewer trees and even these were smaller. Marking a trail was difficult. Ted wondered about the scarcity of vegetation. He mentioned it to the young man who was acting as their guide.

"Oh, can't you understand that? Why we're reaching the timber line. You see vegetation can only grow a certain distance up on the mountains. Usually to about nine or ten thousand feet. And up here you'll find the temperature a lot colder than down in the canyons. Now are you beginning to understand why they insisted on your bringing along some heavier clothing?"

"I sure am," Ted exclaimed. "And I'm beginning to understand that gnawing feeling in the pit of my stomach. I'm hungry. It must be past noon. How about us stopping and having a bite?"

"Sure," the guide said. "I was thinking the same thing. But you want to go as easy on your food as possible. You know that it's going to have to last for some time."

"Yeah," Pudge said brightly, "but if we eat it all now, we won't have such a load to carry. That makes sense, doesn't it?"

"It might make sense to some people," Ted said. "But not to me. We'll need all our strength coming back down this grade and we can't feel too good if we gobble all our food now."

Pudge grinned sheepishly as he climbed down off his mount. "Okay, okay. I always give in to you—because you're usually right." Pudge tied the horse to a small, stunted pine. Soon they had a fire going. They fried bacon and made bacon sandwiches. They also had milk in cup containers and a small can of fruit which they divided. They had been carrying their food in a small bundle.

Now Pudge suggested, "That food is important. So are our flares and gun. I tell you what. We can unroll our blankets and pack all of that stuff together. Ted, if you'll carry my frying pan and eating equipment, I'll roll the other stuff in my blanket. That way, we'll do away with an extra package."

"Good idea," Ted commented. "The easier we can have it, the better things will work out for us. Now let's see. I'll give you the flares and the rifle. We can unbolt the rifle and it will come in half so that it will be easy to carry. Here are a few cans of food and the bread that can also go in your roll. If the things get too heavy for you, I'll carry them awhile."

Lunch completed, the two youths did not waste much time. Ted continued to mark trail up the steep, rock-strewn ascent, while the heavier Pudge rode behind his guide. After another hour of weaving in and out among the rocks, they reached the top of the rise. Now they were truly above the timber line. They could see far below them into the valleys and canyons. They saw hundreds of tiny lakes that dotted the landscape with star-studded brilliance. It was a beautiful sight, one that made the rough journey worth the trouble. But they could not tarry.

"We've made good time," the guide said. "But we still have quite a piece of traveling to do. We'll follow this ridge for another mile, then we start up that peak over there."

"Say . . . that peak has snow on it," Ted said. "I'll bet this turns out to be a cold night. That old camp-fire will certainly feel good—and, boy, am I glad I thought of that. Pudge, what do people up above the timber line do when they want to build a fire at night to keep warm?"

"Why, they just build one," Pudge grinned. "You know . . . matches, sticks and things . . . catch on?"

"Only if they're above the timber line," Ted said, "how do they find wood? Ever stop to think of that?"

"Oh, my," Pudge muttered in alarm. "No wood . . . oh, oh, what a night we would have put in if you hadn't thought of that."

The guide smiled. "I was wondering if you were going to think of that. Most tenderfeet, when they start up a peak, never stop to wonder what they'll do for wood. Fortunately for you fellows, it won't be neces-sary to turn back for wood. Right now we're on the top of this bald ridge. But you'll notice ahead that when we start up the south side of that peak, there is a bit of scrubby stuff. You often find scrubby trees and things growing on south slopes. That's because the sun strikes them and the snow melts faster, furnishing them with plenty of water. But on the north side of the peak —if you could see it—you would find it quite bare."

The going along the ridge was fairly level for awhile and Ted turned the job of marking trail over to Pudge. They went steadily toward the towering, snow-covered peak. Midafternoon found them entering a canyon that led up the peak. They walked and rode steadily, taking turns laying trail. And finally just before the sun went over the range to the west, they reached a spot beside a narrow trickling mountain stream.

"Well, here we are," the guide said. "You're to pitch your camp here and start back in the morning. You have everything you will possibly need—if you're care-ful. We've made better time than I expected. Since it is going to be a moonlit night and I know the way back, I'll start back to camp with the horses. Good-by. And the best of luck."

The guide turned around and Ted and Pudge stood there, watching him ride out of sight. After the last hoofbeats died out, they turned to stare at each other.

Suddenly, from far away came the mournful howl of a coyote. Ted grinned.

"Well, mountaineer, we're alone at last. We're on our own. Personally, it feels swell to me."

"Me too," Pudge said. "Only," he added thoughtfully, "I'd like it even more if those coyotes would keep quiet. Somehow, they don't make for pleasant dreams. . . ."

13. THROUGH FOREST AND STREAM

AFTER eating a cold supper, due to their desire to conserve their small supply of wood for a warm breakfast, the two young men set about pitching camp. They found, to their chagrin, that they would be unable to use a tree for a tent pole because there simply were no trees in sight.

Darkness descended rapidly. Using their lone flashlight, they found four rocks about a foot square. These they used as corners for their blankets. Half of the blankets were spread out flat on a smooth place and the four rocks were used as weights on the corners, and finally the waterproof sheet was stretched over the rocks. This gave them a space of about a foot in which to sleep, and at the same time it kept the cold air out.

They put the other half of the blankets over them and crawled in. Both young men were tired from the day's long hike and they fell asleep at once. The night was cold and it continued to grow colder. How many hours passed Ted did not know. But suddenly he was awakened by a long, insistent moan. But it was not the moan of a distant wolf as Ted soon discovered. The wind was making the noise. And when Ted stuck his head out, he got the surprise of his young life. He reached over, shook Pudge by the shoulder.

"Pudge . . . Pudge, wake up a minute. We're in a fix."

"Aw," Pudge mumbled, "whuzzamatter? I'm sleepy. I . . . hey, it's cold. Br-rrr! I don't like this a little bit."

"You'll like something else even less," Ted said grimly. "Take a peek outside, will you. How do you like the sight?"

"Snowing!" Pudge grunted. "Well, can you beat that?"

"No, I can't beat it. But I'm not too surprised. We're up high on this peak. Fall is coming along pretty shortly. I've heard of it snowing up here at this time of year."

"Well, turn over and go to sleep then," Pudge growled. "Why wake me up to see the pretty snow-flakes when I can see plenty of them in the morning? That sounds foolish to me."

"Maybe this won't sound quite so foolish," Ted said quietly. "Did you ever stop to think that for the past several miles, our only trail marks have been made with rock? What will happen if this storm covers the markers? Then where are we?"

"On top of a pretty cold mountain," Pudge said

gloomily. "But there's one nice thing about it. We know that to go home, we have to go down. That's something."

Ted sat there for a moment, saying nothing. All desire to sleep had now fled his brain. He knew they could be in a tight spot and he was giving it plenty of thought.

Pudge sat up in bed, too. "Do you really think we might get lost?" Pudge asked.

"Yes . . . yes, I think there is more than a remote possibility. It's snowing hard now. Our best bet is to wait here until morning and start out with daylight. If we can get down past the timber line, maybe there won't be any snow there. They said it would take two days to get back to camp following trail. The thing that worries me is how long it will take if we can't find the trail."

"How do you think I'm going to be able to sleep if you talk like that?" Pudge complained. Then he grinned in the darkness. "I didn't exactly mean that. This is fun, Ted. Imagine being lost in the wilderness like this! I can't wait for morning to come. I want to get out and get started."

"Well, you won't have long to wait. I see faint streaks of light over to the left of us. I'm going to put on my boots and wait until daylight comes."

Pudge joined Ted and together they sat there, staring at the lightening sky. When they were positive that daylight was but a few moments off, they threw off their cover and began to prepare for breakfast. Ted shook the dry snow from the firewood he had gathered the afternoon before. He soon had a fire going.

The sky was overcast when they finished breakfast. The wind was moaning and being high up on top of the world gave the two young campers a desolate feeling. They shivered as they put out the fire with snow, rolled their provisions into their blanket rolls. Snow was still falling. Ted took the lead but after he had gone a hundred steps, he knew that it was no good.

"We may as well admit it," Ted said. "We're not going to be able to see our trail marks. They're completely drifted over. Our only chance is to go back in the direction we came and try to hit the timber line at the same place we came in."

Pudge said, "But try and find where we crossed the timber line! Going back everything looks different. I can't remember passing any of this stuff. And the snow makes it even worse."

Ted could not comment on that. For every word that Pudge had spoken was true. Nothing looked the same. The trail was drifted over and the wind was lashing against their faces. They had no way of knowing how much time was passing. Neither of them owned a watch. They kept going but they made slow time.

"I've got a funny feeling in the pit of my stomach,"

Pudge said. "It must mean that it's noon. Let's stop and eat."

"It might mean something else," Ted said grimly. "It might mean that you're afraid of what's going to happen. Pains in stomachs don't necessarily mean hunger. Fear plays tricks, too."

"I didn't think of that," Pudge muttered. "If that's the case, let's keep pushing ahead. But boy, am I glad that I didn't gobble all that food yesterday. It sounds good, having it now."

They walked for perhaps half an hour, then Ted said, "I don't want to alarm you, Pudge, but if I'm not mistaken, I saw some scrub pine off to the left of us. If that's true, we've reached the timber line. Come on, let's break off in that direction and find out for ourselves."

They hurried off to the left, eagerly, hopefully. Suddenly, Ted pitched forward on his face, landed in a snowdrift. Pudge, who was trailing a step behind, fell over him. "Hey, what's this? You hurt, Ted? You all right?"

"I never felt better," Ted said. "That thing I tripped over was a root. And roots don't grow where there aren't trees or bushes. We're in the timber—or will be shortly if we keep going on down. Get up, my fat friend, and we'll be off."

They scrambled to their feet and once again began to go down the face of a steep cliff. As they walked and scrambled down the rocks, they came to more and more trees. The snow did not seem as thick or as deep as it had been up higher. It was much warmer after they got in the timber.

"We may not be lost," Ted said, "but we've never been down this route before, either. We may as well face it, Pudge. We haven't a ghost of a chance of getting back by following our marks. We'll have to use our homing instinct. Right now, how about stopping for a bite to eat?"

"I've never heard more pleasant words," Pudge admitted.

They sat down. This time, however, they did not take the time to build a fire. They had bread and a cold can of pork and beans. That was enough to sustain them for the rest of the afternoon.

Before they finished with their short snack, however, they found another ray of light. Suddenly, the snow was no longer falling and in a moment the sun was shining and in a small area around it was a patch of blue sky. It was a warming feeling.

Ted looked at the shadow of a tree. By examining the direction the shadow was falling upon the snow, he was able to tell approximately in which direction lay the camp. He knew that they were somewhere west of it and that to get back, they must follow a generally easterly direction.

"I think," Ted said quickly, "that the sun is going

to shine for awhile. How long it will last I don't know. But while it's nice, we'd better be moving on. My idea is to keep going down until we get well into the timber. That will give us protection for tonight and at the same time, the lower we go, the less apt we are to bump into another storm tonight."

They began to move ahead and this time they made speed. They spoke very little. The important thing was to conserve energy. Down and down they went, over rocks and through trees that grew higher and higher as they proceeded. The sun kept creeping over in the sky until it was behind them.

Finally Ted said, "It must be three o'clock. We've made excellent time. I don't think we're in any danger of snow now that we're down this low. We don't know where we're going and there's no use to get frantic. For one, I suggest that we slow down, now that we're temporarily out of danger. I'd like to enjoy this trip since we're now out of the race completely. Those woodcraft points are gone to someone else."

Ted had eased the pack off his back and had taken a seat on a large rock that overlooked a small trickling stream below them. It was now quite warm and the heavy clothes were getting uncomfortable. Pudge seated himself beside Ted, after first removing his pack and putting it on the ledge beside him.

Suddenly, Ted said in a husky whisper, "Pudge, look what we've been missing by going so fast."

Almost directly below them were half a dozen beavers. The energetic little animals were busy working on a dam. They were packing mud against a log that had fallen across the stream.

"Look at those furry little fellows work," Pudge exclaimed softly. "Did you ever see anything like it? And see the way they gnawed that tree down. It's as clean a job as you could do with a saw."

"It sure is," Ted agreed, grinning. "I wonder if they'd keep working that way if they knew we were watching them?" Ted lapsed into thoughtful silence then.

Ted gave one last look at the beaver pond below him. Then he started jogging on down the path. Pudge got up to follow him and as he did so he accidentally knocked his bed roll into the beaver pond and it immediately sank deep down, out of sight.

Ted and Pudge raced down the bank. Ted reached the beaver dam first. He stood staring down into the water. It was clear, but the shadows were falling upon it and it was impossible to see the bottom at that point. He rolled up his sleeve as high as he could, lay down flat upon his stomach and reached down.

"I can't feel a thing," he said gloomily. "It's deeper than I thought. Maybe we can find something to feel around with."

Ted took his hatchet, found a small dead pine that was about ten feet high. He cut it down quickly, peeled the limbs off it. He then had a nice long pole. But to his surprise, when he thrust the pole into the water, it was impossible to reach bottom.

"I can't feel a thing," he announced. "But there is an undertow down there. I can feel the pull of the water against this stick. Pudge, we have to face the fact squarely. The bed roll and all it contained is lost."

"That doesn't sound so promising," Pudge said. "We can't possibly signal anyone now. We haven't our flares and we haven't a gun. That means just one thing. Either we find our way out of this jungle alone—or we don't get out."

They got back up to the level on which they had been walking. Now Ted was in the lead again. They had walked perhaps a mile when Ted said, "Take a look at this rock formation."

They were passing a huge boulder of granite. The boulder had a crevice near the bottom. Ted shone his flashlight into the crevice.

"A cave," Pudge commented. "Looks to me that as long as we're short on bedding it would be a good idea to climb in there and get out of the weather. How about it, Ted?"

"We still have half an hour of light. Or maybe even a bit longer. We can make good mileage in that time. Come on. Let's push on."

They hurried on. Ted kept marking the trail. They

went around the side of the canyon, entered another one. Ted decided they were going in the wrong direction so he changed his course. The sun had gone beyond the range now and in a while, darkness would descend. Ted said, "We can go for perhaps ten more minutes. I'm mixed up. Which direction shall we try? Your guess is as good as mine."

"That way," Pudge said, pointing to the left. So again they began to follow the contour of the hill. Darkness was almost upon them.

They stopped. Ted shone his flashlight around. "I'll pick out a dead tree," he said, "and build a fire."

"With what?" Pudge demanded. "The matches are in the lost bed roll."

Suddenly, Ted called back to Pudge.

"Look! Here's one of our trail marks. We're back on our old trail! We've stumbled onto it. What blind luck!"

"Hooray!" shouted Pudge in return.

Once again, they started out.

They rounded a curve in the trail. There was something vaguely familiar about the whole thing. And suddenly Ted knew what it was. He pointed ahead with his flashlight.

"Pudge . . . give a look, you'll feel like kicking yourself."

Pudge Lawson looked and what he saw made him emit a low, mournful groan. "My gosh," he said.

"That's the cave we passed this afternoon. Why—we've been going around in a circle!"

"I don't know what else could be wrong," Pudge said gloomily. "We're lost. We've been going in circles. We have no food, no matches—not even enough bedding to keep warm. What's more, we have no way of signalling or of protecting ourselves. The only nice thing about the whole thing is the fact that we do have a cave to sleep in."

They stepped into the cave. It was nice and dry and while the ceiling wasn't high, it was enough to shelter them. The cave extended back into the mountain, but the passage was small and because Ted remembered the last time he had crawled through an underground passage, he made up his mind that he would not try to explore this one. He was flashing his light around the walls when an idea struck him. He walked over to one of the walls, examined a streak of white that ran through the rock. Suddenly he decided that he might be right. He took his knife, began to pry the white loose. He chipped away two small white rocks, held them in his hand.

"See these two white rocks. All right, watch me when I turn out my flashlight." Ted snapped off the light and then rubbed the two rocks together. They gave off a sheet of flame that was a great deal like lightning.

"This is flint rock," Ted said. "I used to pick it up off the river banks back home."

"I suppose you're going to sit around and play with the flint all night," Pudge groaned, "while I try to sleep. What a sense of humor you have."

"Come on. We're going outside and gather some leaves and pine cones. Then we want some dead logs. If I know anything about woodcraft, we're about to have a fire."

In ten minutes they had an adequate supply of wood. They placed the leaves in a cleared space, then piled the pine cones loosely on top of them. It was at that moment that Ted reached into his pocket.

"This little thing here," he said, holding a small, round object up proudly in front of him, "is a rifle shell. I just happened to have it in my clothes and it might be the luckiest thing that ever happened to us. Look, Pudge. I'm going to open this bullet. There is a small amount of powder in it. See, I'm sprinkling the powder down over the leaves. If we're lucky, we'll have a fire. Okay, you hold the flashlight."

"That's not all I'm holding," Pudge said. "The most important thing I'm holding right now is my breath."

Ted's fingers were shaking as he held the two pieces of flint apart. Then, swiftly, he brushed them together. There was a burst of fire—then a minor explosion as the powder caught on and then the fire was started. Soon they had a merry blaze and it was so cheerful they decided to put on enough wood to keep it burning all night.

"Boy, oh boy," Pudge said. "If I just had something to eat right now, I'd be the happiest guy on earth."

"Maybe," Ted said thoughtfully, "we'll have something to eat for breakfast. We managed to get a fire burning. Surely there's a way of figuring out how to get something to eat."

They sat around the fire a long time, each of them lost in his own thoughts. Finally Ted said, "We may as well turn in . . ." Ted stopped right then, for the woods suddenly rang with the ominous cry of a wolf. The wolf was nearby, too. "As a matter of fact," Ted added hastily, "the sooner we get into that cave the better I'm going to like it."

They went inside. A moment later, the cry of the wolf came again. This time, it was even closer. Suddenly, Ted gave a start. "Do you know what? We're in that wolf's den. This is where he sleeps. Quick, help me with this rock. We'll shove it in front of the entrance."

They did that and the moan of the wolf was not quite so loud. "Well," Ted said, "we know the wolf can't get in. He can sit out there until doomsday and he still won't get us."

"Yeah," Pudge said. "That's what's worryin' me. He's apt to sit out there until doomsday—and that will keep us from leaving this place."

"Maybe he'll go away before long," Ted said hopefully.

But Ted was wrong. The wolf didn't go away. He sat not too far out of the circle of light of the camp fire. And all night long he wailed at short intervals. When morning came, neither of them had slept. The question then was: Was it safe to leave, or had the wolf remained outside, waiting for them? The only way to learn was to go outside and see.

"I'll try it first," Ted offered. "But you don't know how much I'd give to have that old rifle in my hands at this minute."

Carefully then, and with his breath driving through him unaccountably fast, Ted Moran eased the rock back, away from the small, doorlike entrance. He peered out. All seemed to be serene. The sun had come out and now the remnants of yesterday's storm had disappeared. Boldly then, Ted stepped outside. Nothing attacked him. There was no sound, save the gurgling of the water.

"Pudge—come on out here," Ted exclaimed.

Pudge crawled through the entrance, stood there, stretching. But suddenly he said, "Did you think of a way of getting us something to eat?"

"I'm about to think of it," Ted said. "What do we need to rig up a pole and line?"

"The first thing we need is a pole," Pudge said.

"All right," Ted answered eagerly. "We need a pole. So we take our knife and cut a long sapling. Then we peel the bark off of it and we have a tough, limber pole

that will do in the emergency. Now the next thing we
need is a line."

Pudge's face fell. "For a minute," he muttered, "I
thought you had something. I haven't got a ball of
string in my pocket and I'm sure that you're past the
string-carrying age yourself."

"But if we had string," Ted persisted, "all we would
need then would be a hook of some kind. And we can
make a hook, Pudge. That souvenir camp pin that
you've got in your tie. All we have to do is bend it into
the shape of a hook. We'd have to disguise the hook to
look like a fly. Let's see. Something bright. A yellow
color or red, perhaps."

Pudge was again evidencing interest. His eyes looked
all around and suddenly he blurted, "Your sock, Ted.
The red tops are made of yarn and they're sticking up
over your boots. Do you suppose they'd unravel if you
started them right?"

Ted started a run in his yarn socks with his knife.
He gave the loose end a jerk and to his surprise, the
stocking began to unravel. He had jerked off perhaps
ten feet when Pudge said, "Now I get it. You're going
to try to use the yarn for a line. Well, it looks like good
tough yarn. It might work."

"You build up a fire," Ted ordered. "I'm going to
look for a feather from a bird's wing." In ten minutes
Ted was back with the feather which he had found on
the ground under a tree.

He took Pudge's tie pin, then bent it into the shape of a hook. He wrapped the hook with yarn, then splitting the feather, he tied the two pieces to the hook. The result was a rather crude-looking fly. But it was bright and Ted hoped it might fool a trout. He tied the unravelled yarn to the end of the hook, then fastened the other end to the pole.

Ted and Pudge walked down to the stream's edge. Then Ted whipped the fly above the place where the water churned down over the rock. The fly sped swiftly downstream, then was sucked into the churning spray. For an instant the red yarn was invisible. Then there was a swift tug on the line. A speckled brook trout leaped high out of the water and the yarn all but parted. There was no time to play the trout for the danger of the yarn breaking was great. So Ted, crossing his fingers for luck, gave a jerk and the trout was yanked up out of the water and came sailing toward the bank. The trout had come off the hook. It alighted close to the water's edge, but upon the rocks. Pudge leaped for it, fell upon the wriggling beauty and smothered it with his body.

The trout was a nice one. It weighed a good pound. While Pudge dressed it, Ted pulled the line from the makeshift pole and wrapped it so that it could be used again. They ate the fish and the broth and when they finished, they felt much better. After putting out the fire they again started off down the mountain. This time Ted did not attempt to mark trail for yesterday it had led him in a complete circle—a thing that was quite simple to do in the mountains. Many men, experienced in mountain travel, have found themselves back at the starting point after days of continuous walking.

"I'm remembering something that Indian Jim told me," Ted said after they had walked a while. "It was about water and the way it flows. We know one thing, Pudge. Water flows downhill and we're going downhill now. This stream is a small one. If we follow it, it will empty into a larger stream and that larger stream will empty into an even larger one. If we keep going along the stream, we can't help finding civilization of some kind. Are you willing to chance it?"

"Sounds good to me," Pudge said. "At least we'll have all the water we want to drink and that's something. Besides, the way you caught that brook trout was so simple that I'd hate to get away from the only source of food we have."

Thus began the tedious journey along the bank of the stream. Rounding a bend in the stream, they came out to a rather prominent rock ledge. The river disappeared over the ledge in a waterfall. And below the ledge was a lake that was at least half a mile across.

"You know," Ted mused, "the lake at the camp is connected to a whole string of smaller lakes. I'm wondering if this can't be one of those lakes? If it is, then we could go from one lake to the other and eventually find ourselves back in camp. It's a gamble, risking it— but we have to gamble now."

"It sounds reasonable," Pudge admitted soberly. "But how could we ever get across these lakes? We haven't a boat and we can't carve one with a hatchet and a hunting knife."

"Follow me," Ted said at last. "I've got a hunch that we can rig up something."

Pudge got up, followed Ted as the latter made his way down the perilous cliff beside the waterfall. After fifteen or twenty minutes of herculean effort, they reached the bottom. But Ted did not stop to rest. Along the shore of the lake were dozens of pieces of driftwood. Ted set about searching for logs of a certain size. He found the first one. It was about six inches through the middle and about eight feet in length.

"Now," Ted said, "if we can find about ten more of these, I think we can build a raft. It won't be much of a raft—but it might float if we can get it to hold together. You look for more logs like this one. In the meantime I'm going to find something we can use to bind the logs together."

Ted walked back up the slope a bit. He came to a young sapling about ten feet high. He cut it off at the base. Then using his hunting knife, he made a cut from one end of the tree to the other. The sapling was green. It was a matter of but a few moments until Ted had peeled the bark cleanly from the tree. He then tore the bark into bands about an inch wide. The bands were supple and they were strong. Ted cut down two more saplings and made more of the strips of green bark. He went back to where Pudge was and found that his companion had found the necessary logs to build the raft. Then fastening the ends of the bark together, Ted had a long, ropelike strip. He began to weave it in and out around the ends of the logs, binding them securely together. Then to make the raft sturdier, he braced the ends with smaller logs and tied them securely. It was nearing dusk when they finished their task. Their fingers were blistered from the hard work, but they surveyed their handiwork with pride that was justifiable. Carefully they placed round logs under the raft and using the logs for rollers, shoved the craft into the lake. It floated evenly and the two youths gave a spontaneous shout.

Pudge said, "Let's get some dry logs that we can split. While we're riding, we may as well try to make some crude paddles." This they did, then as darkness became a reality, the two friends pushed out into the lake.

14. FIRE IN THE WILDERNESS

TED and Pudge were never to forget that night. The stars above them were shining like a thousand bright lights. The moon lighted the shore line until it looked as clear as day. But there was a wind. A lashing mountain wind that swept from a northwest direction and chilled them through. They dared not try to go to sleep on the raft.

They shielded themselves against the icy blasts as best they could. Ted chopped at one of the logs with his hatchet. By the time the moon was halfway across the sky, he had fashioned a rather rude-looking paddle. He gave the hatchet to Pudge and before Pudge was finished with his paddle, they had drifted across the lake and were entering a small stream again. Ted paddled slowly, kept the raft between the banks of the stream. And just as he had hoped, they entered a lake on the other side of the first one. This lake seemed in the darkness to be smaller than the first had been. Finally Pudge got his paddle fashioned so that he could use it. Pudge moved up to the front and began to paddle evenly, steadily.

Morning found them crossing the fourth lake. They were tired and nearer the point of exhaustion than they had been during the whole trip. But they kept grimly on. The lakes were growing closer together, smaller. Suddenly, they paddled through a cut and emerged upon a large lake.

"Ahead," shouted Ted, "is the sweetest sight these eyes of mine ever saw. Camp ahoy! We're back at last."

They were halfway across the lake when Pudge said, "They've sighted us. Look at them running down toward the shore. There's Indian Jim. He's jumping into a canoe. He's going to come out and get us."

Indian Jim did come out. He met the two youths before they could reach shore. He grunted somberly, but Ted could tell that the Indian was glad to see them. "Tenderfeet stay long," Jim said. "Camp worry much." Then Jim's eyes fell upon the raft and a smile crossed his red face. "Tenderfeet do good job."

Indian Jim motioned them into his canoe. The boys transferred their belongings into the sleek craft, then seated themselves in the bow. Jim propelled them back to shore with swift, deft strokes of his paddle. When they disembarked, they found half the camp gathered on the shore, waiting for them.

"Welcome back," Jeff Jones said, extending an outstretched hand to them. "You don't know how glad we are to see you. You were the only ones who didn't get home last night."

"We had a storm," Ted said. "It covered our trail. . . ."

"Some of the others had the same trouble," the camp director said. "But they used their flares and rescue was sent out for them. The boys who went south escaped the storm. They made the best time."

"You fellows look pretty well done in," the camp director told them. "Come on up and get something to eat. You must have run out of food a bit early."

Ted nudged Pudge. Now that it was over, they could see the amusing side of it. "You don't know the half of it," Ted grinned. But later after they had eaten, it was not as easy to grin. For they were standing in front of the bulletin board, staring at the new point totals. Lem and Rocky had indeed won the woodcraft points by arriving back at camp in record time. The score as far as Ted and Rocky were concerned was:

Rocky: 360   Ted: 239

"Well, it was a good race while it lasted," Ted admitted dolefully.

Early that afternoon Ted and Pudge went to bed to catch up on the sleep they had lost. Ted fell asleep almost the minute he climbed into bed. In the middle of that night, his sleep was interrupted by a piercing shriek. Ted jumped up from his bunk. As he did so, he saw the strange red glow through a west window. Then the shriek came again. A camper thrust his head into the door.

"Forest fire! All hands out at once to fight the fire."

Ted's desire for sleep vanished at once. He was out of bed in a flash. Pudge was a step behind him. They climbed into their clothes, questions surging from their lips.

One thing was evident the moment they got outside. The canyon to the west of them was one glowing mass of flame. The brown smoke was billowing up in huge clouds. The crackling of burning wood could be plainly heard.

Campers were scampering about in every direction. Someone shouted, "Jeff Jones rode up to halfway house on horseback. He had some important mail to send out. He won't be back until almost morning. I think Indian Jim went with him. What can we do?"

The fire was sweeping down the canyon and at that time, it appeared to be about half a mile away. Suddenly Rocky Stone jumped up and stood atop a camp table in the center of the clearing.

"Let me have your attention!" Rocky shouted loudly. There was no mistaking the authoritative tone of his voice. It commanded silence and immediately the other campers gathered around him. This was not the old Rocky speaking, but a new Rocky. A confident Rocky in the face of approaching danger.

"Men, we can't possibly fight that fire with water. We haven't enough. I've been through a forest fire before and I know what a job it is. Now quickly. Split into two sections."

Ted could not help but admire Rocky for the way he was taking charge, for the grim efficiency with which he took hold of the situation. "There's an old saying— fight fire with fire. Well, that's our only chance. The fire is burning this way. Because of the snow up high, I think the fire will burn itself out up high. We have to stop it before it gets here. Quick, all of you find gunny sacks. Wet them. When that's done, come back here and be prepared to fight."

Gunny sacks were found in the stables—sacks that had been used for feed. They were quickly wetted down and the young men were back, anxiously await- ing the next order.

"Now half of you," Rocky said, "are to go around back of the camp. The other half is to stay here. I'll take gasoline and matches and start the blazes. The idea is this: I'm going to light a row of fires that will extend half around the camp. From this side, we're going to keep it put out. The purpose will be for the fire we start to burn away from camp. After awhile our fire will meet the one coming down this way. Then it will burn out. All right, get going. I'm beginning my fire at once."

Ted and Pudge were in the group that followed

Rocky toward the west side of camp. Rocky had a tin
of gasoline. He started to pour it along the ground
beneath the evergreens. Then he struck a match to it
and a row of trees, about thirty yards long, immediately began to go up in flames. Rocky went on, ig-
niting strips, then moving on around the camp.

Ted and Pudge began to beat the ground furiously.
The heat of the crackling flames was intense. It singed
the hair on their arms. Sparks flew at them, burned
tiny holes in their clothes. Their feet were soon hot
from the scorching ground. The wind brought billowing smoke across the clearing back of them. It choked
them; yet they stayed there, swinging the sacks, pounding out the fire that threatened to creep down upon the
camp. All around the camp, in a half circle, the fire was
glowing redly. And young men, some of them stripped
bare to the waist, were struggling heroically to keep
the flames back. It was a grim struggle they were wag-
ing. The flames would leap from tree to tree. A spark
would be carried by the wind, would drop in the grassy
clearing and the fire would spring up there. Time
after time, a fighter would have to leave his post to
come into the clearing and beat out the beginning of
a fire there. But gradually they were checking the blaze.
And in the opposite direction they could see their own
fire eating a blazing course toward the other one.

They fought the fire until dawn. By then the danger

of it burning the camp had passed. Jeff Jones arrived at that time. He looked the situation over, then said, "You've saved the camp. But the wind has changed. The fire is swinging out around the lake. We've got to stop it. We've got to!"

15. TO THE RESCUE

TED MORAN listened to the words of the camp director. And listening alone was enough to cause him to
shudder. For he was thinking that if the fire swung out
wide enough, it would indeed envelop the shack of
the Prospector—and Old Prospector, still weak from
his sickness, might not see it in time to get away.

"The only way to stop this fire," the camp director
said, "is to go straight across the lake and backfire.
We'll lose timber all around the lake—but it can't be
helped. Come on, at least half of you. We'll set up fires
and try to keep them under control and sweeping this
way. The rangers will be working to the east of us.
They will be able to organize patrols that will stop the
fire from moving in that direction. As for the rest of
you, you are under the direct charge of Rocky Stone.
He has done a masterful job so far. I'm giving him full
authority to do as he sees fit."

There was a chorus of agreement. Then Jeff Jones
moved off with half the group. In the group that re-

mained was Ted as well as his sidekick, Pudge. They
were dog-tired from the night of fighting flame. But
they could not think of that now. They followed Rocky
into the burned area. They came upon the place where
the fire was still burning, where it was sweeping out
around the camp. It was there that they began to fight
it.

Some of the campers used axes. They would cut
down dead trees and live ones as well, dragging them
into the path of the flames. Then they took up their
posts in the clearing and kept the fire from jumping to
the other trees. It was a battle where life and death
hung in the balance.

Noon came. Huge billows of smoke shot skyward.
But by then the fire was around on the back side of the
camp and it was evident they would be able to keep
it under control—if the wind didn't shift again. Far
to the east they could see more smoke and that cheered
them. Apparently the forest rangers had gotten their
fire patrols organized. For this smoke meant that back-
firing was going on. And on the north shore of the
lake there was another blaze. It was sweeping around
the lake toward them. The back side of the fire seemed
to be under control—a fact that spoke well for the
courageous fighters under the direction of the camp
director. It looked as if the fires would meet sometime
before nightfall. But that was what worried Ted. Before the fires met, they would have had to burn over

the very shack that housed Old Prospector. Suddenly Ted made his decision. He was but a minor cog in the fire-fighting equipment now. One man, more or less, should not be too vital in stemming the fire. But as an individual he still might have time to get to the Prospector's shack and rescue the old man if he were in trouble.

So Ted threw down his sack, began to race down the hill. But he heard a shout behind him. A hoarse, commanding shout. "Wait, Moran. Where are you going? Get back here!" It was Rocky Stone and Rocky was shouting angrily. "Get back here, I say!"

But Ted kept running. Of course, he knew that he could be charged with deserting his post. He probably would be, for that matter—but he had weighed the situation from every side. What was the breaking of a rule when human life was involved? He had no time to stop and explain things. For already he could see that the fire had swept up over the hill back of Prospector's house. The crackling of flames was to Ted's ears a veritable sound of doom.

He reached the water's edge. There was a canoe handy and Ted leaped into it. Swiftly then he began to paddle straight toward the opposite bank. It was a mile—a cruel distance to paddle at full speed.

Halfway across the lake, Ted's breath was coming through his parched throat in searing, agonizing gasps. His muscles were crying from the fatigue. Yet he

grimly kept his resolution to rescue Prospector if it
were humanly possible to do so.

But was it? The flames, clearly visible now, were
rolling down the hill toward the old stone shack, rolling like a tumbleweed before a storm. They were cruel-
looking things, those tongues of fire. Anxiously, Ted
redoubled his efforts. He drove the paddle into the
water in a sprint stroke. He would close his eyes and
when he opened them again, the bank would seem
even farther away than it had before. But eventually
he made it. The prow of his boat slammed against a
log. Ted jumped out, raced up the hill. His heart fell
at the sight that met his vision.

The cabin was enveloped in flames! Every tree
around it was burning. And nothing but the tin roof
was keeping the cabin from going up in smoke. There
was a cloud of smoke and flame all about the cabin.
Ted Moran whirled around, raced back to the lake. He
jumped in, wetted his clothes thoroughly. Then climb-
ing out, he put his wet arm in front of his face, set
himself for his race with death. Into the roaring in-
ferno he charged. His wet boots made little sizzling
noises against the hot embers. His shoulder hit the
Prospector's door. Wood splintered under the lunge.
Ted bolted inside the cabin. There writhing in agony
upon the bed was the Prospector. He was near un-
consciousness and he was choking for breath in the
dense smoke. Ted took a sheet from the bed, jammed

it down in the water bucket. Then swiftly he wrapped it around the old man's face. He lifted Prospector to his shoulders and once again plunged into the sheet of flame.

The race to the beach took an eternity. Ted stumbled, choked in the smoke, but he did not fall with his human cargo. At last they reached the dock. But it was only to find it a mass of blazing flame. The paint on the prow of the canoe was curling under the heat. Ted deposited Prospector in the bottom of the canoe, shoved away from shore. He paddled out a few yards so that they were out of the heat. Then he turned the Prospector over on his stomach in the bottom and began to work on him.

It seemed queer to Ted that this was just a repetition of what had happened the first time he met Prospector. Then the old man had been half drowned and Ted had applied the artificial breathing method to revive him. Now it was smoke that filled the old man's lungs instead of water—but both were equally dangerous. He worked swiftly and efficiently, but to no avail.

The main body of fire passed over the spot where the cabin was located. It swept on toward camp—toward the other fire that was burning back in the opposite direction. Soon the fires would meet and burn out —for there was no place else to burn. The fire patrols had done superhuman work—had backfired so effectively that only a small part of the forest's natural beauty would be ruined. But Ted Moran knew none of this. He was too busy working over the inert old man in the canoe.

Minutes lengthened into an hour. Two hours . . . and then a show of natural color on the old man's neck. "Prospector. Do you hear me, Prospector?" Perspiration was beading along Ted's furrowed brow.

The old man turned over. His eyelids fluttered and to the corners of his mouth came a weak smile. "H-hello, youngster." The old Prospector stopped a moment, got his breath. Ted helped him to a sitting position, reached over and with cupped hands, got some cool water which he splashed in his face.

Prospector smiled again, said, "I—I must have gotten too much smoke. You—you saved me again, youngster. I'll never be able to pay my debt to you."

"Forget it," Ted commanded. "Now don't talk. You're all in. I see where your stone shack has been saved because of the tin roof. The fire's almost burned out around it. I'll take you back there temporarily. But I'm going to ask the camp director if we can't bring you over to camp and take care of you until you get to feeling better. . . ."

"Y-you'd do that for me, youngster? Even if it got you into trouble? You know what they told you about me."

"It isn't a question of right or wrong," Ted said

firmly. "I'm right. And as quickly as I can get back there, I'll talk to Jeff Jones about you. He can't refuse to take you in."

Ted began to paddle leisurely back toward shore. The day had almost passed. It was time to get back to camp. Just as he beached the canoe, a trout jumped out of the water beside the boat. It wasn't too large. Only about fourteen inches long. But it reminded Ted of the fishing award points. In a few days camp would be over—and his dream of being Gold Star Camper ended.

Prospector must have seen Ted looking that way, for he said, "I swear—you got an awful doleful face for a youngster. What's eatin' you?"

Ted told him. Suddenly the old man grinned, "Didn't I tell you not to worry? I'm gonna help you catch that Brown Beauty if I never get another thing done. Did you see that trout leap out? Well, I saw what he was after. A dragonfly that had lit on the water. Look, there's another one flyin' around. Now he's lit. Watch him a minute—there, didn't I tell you. A trout gobbled him up. That means that right now dragonflies are the best bait. They're bigger than other flies, too—and they oughta catch bigger fish. Now I ain't aimin' to go back in that stuffy cabin for awhile. Not until I breathe some of that smoke outa my lungs. So I'll tell you what. Go up there and get my fishin' rod. It's hangin' in a rack above the door. In the corner you'll find a box of flies. Bring 'em all. It's gonna be a nice evenin' and you and me'll just go fishin'."

"Look, Prospector, I'd love to go," Ted said. "But you aren't in any condition to go. You've been a sick man."

"Which is better," Prospector demanded. "A hot, smoke-filled cabin or fresh air? Now you be sensible yourself. Nothin's gonna harm me out here. I can sit up and swing a paddle every now and then to keep the canoe headed straight. I got an idea about that big fish and we're tryin' it out pronto."

The old man's persuasiveness won Ted over. He decided there was logic in what Old Prospector said. So he hurried up to the cabin. He found the fishing line and the flies. The cabin was warm, for the fire had heated the roof and the stone exterior. Ted threw open the windows so that the place would air out.

Then he hurried back down to the canoe. Prospector was sitting up in the back of the canoe. He held a paddle. Ted started to take it but the old man waved him away.

"I ain't gonna paddle much. Just enough to keep us driftin'. You see, Ted, I got a theory about that rascally old fish. Every night the big fish come in close to the rocky shore where they feed on bugs and little fish. They lay around in the shallow water at night and in deep water in the daytime. Now here's what —I'll keep the canoe out about thirty feet from shore.

You whip your fly into every likely lookin' little spot. Tonight the trout are bitin'. I can feel it in my bones. Besides, didn't you see that one go for that dragonfly?"

"You mean you think that if we go all around the lake, we'll be almost sure to find Brown Beauty?" Ted asked.

"That's exactly it. And I'm willin' to bet that if you can drop that dragonfly within three or four feet of where he's waitin' that you'll have a fish on your hands. That line you're usin' is fifty pound test. Brown Beauty might snag it. But on a steady pull, he ain't got the strength to break it. Well, I ain't gonna sit here talkin' all night. You know what we're gonna do and you're the guy that's doin' the fishin'. So I'd get started if I was you."

Ted tied the fly to suit his fancy. Then gazing critically at it, he decided it was all right. He raised his arm and cast out the line. It was almost his last chance to get Brown Beauty.

16. A VICTORY AND A DEFEAT

Tᴇᴅ had learned that on that particular mountain lake the largest fish were usually caught during the hotter days. He realized that the days were getting cooler and that summer was almost gone. Unless he caught Brown Beauty and caught the fish quickly, there seemed little likelihood that he would ever catch the fish.

Now on his first cast Ted anxiously watched the result. The dragonfly lure landed with a light slap against a little ripple of water. The ripple carried the fly up against the rock shore. Then slowly Ted began to reel in. His nerves were taut, his breath was coming swiftly. In his mind was the thought that at any second a veritable tornado might hit the end of his line. But he reeled the fly clear into the boat's edge without getting a strike. Ted was not downhearted . . . not yet. For he had only cast his fly once. What could you tell after one cast? Or half a dozen, for that matter?

So eagerly he began to whip the shore line. The day ended and the moon came out bright. Ted had dried

195

out completely from his wetting and he took off his
jacket, gave it to Prospector for the old man had been
thinly clad.

Ted didn't miss a single cranny of that shore line.
Prospector would point the canoe toward a spot and
Ted would whip his line out over the bow, or the front
end, and wait for a strike. But the strike didn't come.
Half an hour passed, lengthened into an hour, and then
two. Half a dozen casts became half a hundred. But it
was no use. If there were trout in the lake, they simply
weren't rising to Ted's lure.

They were more than halfway around the lake. Ted's
arm ached from the constant up-and-around motions,
but he set his teeth as his arm flashed over again. The
line lengthened out, hit with a light slap next to a dark
rock on the shore line. There was a fallen tree near the
rock and Ted carefully drew the line back so that the
fly floated past the submerged tree. One moment the
fly was in plain sight. The next minute it had vanished.

Then all of a Fourth-of-July fireworks celebration
seemed to break loose. There came a loud splash as
a huge fish slapped its tail against the water. Next the
fish leaped high into the air and in the light of the pale
moon his sleek, scaly sides glistened with all the lu-
minosity of a Roman candle being shot off. Ted and
Prospector shouted almost as one person.

"Brown Beauty! It's Brown Beauty!"

And so it was. There was no mistaking it. For here was a fish that was far larger than any other that had ever been seen in the lake. Here was a German Brown trout of tremendous proportions. A trout that stood on its tail upon the water and shook at the hook in a manner that made the trout appear to be dancing.

What a superb fighter Brown Beauty was! First the fish plummeted to the depths. But Ted, sitting in the prow of the canoe with his knees locked against the gunnels, was not giving the trout a second of rest. He kept every inch of the slack out of the line. When Brown Beauty tired of pulling on the line, the fish turned and came charging back toward the craft. But Prospector was a fisherman. Skillfully he guessed the direction of the fish's glide and pulled the boat around out of the fish's path. Sure enough, the fish passed in front of the canoe. Had it gone underneath before Ted could have gotten into position, the line might have caught on the bottom of the craft and broken into two pieces—with the big wriggling prize on the wrong piece.

But that danger had been averted. Brown Beauty was now in open water. The fish was so heavy, so fierce in its fight, that gradually the canoe was being pulled back in the direction from which it had come. Ted sat there keeping the slack out, winding in furiously, letting out again, just as the case demanded.

When the trout would break water, exclamations

of delight would burst from Ted's and Prospector's lips. The fish was a beauty—and a gallant old fighter who refused to give up.

But eventually there had to be an end to it. So skillfully did Ted fight that the fish could find no way to break loose. Gradually the mad gyrations lessened in intensity. The leaps out of the water became less and less spirited. Prospector, watching the progress of the battle, skillfully edged the canoe into a small, sandy stretch of beach where the trout could more easily be taken from the water.

Ted climbed out onto the bank, reeled the trout into shallow water. Then with his fingers mentally crossed, he gave one final jerk and the fish was lying upon the bank, flopping and wriggling. But Brown Beauty was not to get away. Not after Ted had waited a whole summer to make such a prize catch. It took him but a moment to run a stick through the fish's mouth and gills. Then taking the fishing line he braided three strands of it into a rope. Leaving the stick through Brown Beauty's mouth so that he could not be bitten by the sharp teeth, Ted thrust the rope · through the gills and brought it out through the mouth. He then knotted it securely and tied the other end to the stern of the canoe.

That way Brown Beauty was returned to the water and there was little danger of the fish dying. Ted took

over the paddle. He paddled swiftly back to Prospector's shack. The old man was rather exhausted
after the work and excitement. Ted walked along with
him to his shack. They found the shack much cooler
than it had been.

Ted said, "I'm going to get them to bring you over
to camp for a few days, Prospector. That way you'll
have all the care you need."

"I'm going to be all right," the old man stated firmly.
"You just run along now and show them that fish. I
reckon you can use them points, eh, youngster?"

"I sure can," Ted grinned. "Thanks to you."

Ted waved a cheery good-by, then went back to his
canoe. He wasted no time in paddling across the lake.
He noted on the way that the fire had almost burned
itself out. There were several trees still afire, but they
were being watched, no doubt, by the fire patrols of the
ranger service.

Ted walked up to camp, carrying his fish with him.
His entrance was like tossing out a bombshell. When
the others saw the huge fish, they were ecstatic in their
praise. All of them except Rocky Stone. Rocky realized how much this would mean to Ted. But even
Rocky seemed more mellowed than he had been. Ted
believed he understood that. In the stress of the fire,
the better element in him had asserted itself. Rocky
Stone would probably always be positive in his man-

ner. But Ted felt that he would never be as unfair about things as he had once been. That part of Rocky seemed to have gone up with the timber.

Jeff Jones said, upon seeing the fish, "That's Brown Beauty, all right. I tell you, boys, this ends the contest as far as I am concerned. There's no doubt that Ted has won first position. And in my mind no one will catch larger trout than Rex Lawrence and Rocky Stone have already caught. So if it's all right with you fellows, I'll put up the points as they now stand."

"It's okay with me," Rocky said. Rex Lawrence nodded assent. As for Ted, he had no argument to offer. He was satisfied in his own mind that he was the winner—that no one could beat him. He got a certain amount of satisfaction seeing the point score go up:

Rocky: 410   Ted: 330

Of course, he realized that he had lost. For there was only one event remaining—the track meet. Even if he won first in the meet, he would have only three hundred and eighty points. But even though he was going to lose, he felt that his summer had been worthwhile.

He had lived in the great out of doors. He had learned to be self-reliant. He had proved time and again that it never pays to quit. Too, there was the sun tan that he would take home, the extra pounds of muscle that had so quietly added to the size of his shoulders and chest. No, he couldn't feel too bad.

The moment the points went up and the contest was declared officially over, Ted took Brown Beauty and started down toward the lake. "Ted . . . Ted, you aren't going to throw Brown Beauty back, are you?" Pudge Lawson demanded.

"Of course, I am," Ted said. "And why not? Think of the dozens of fishermen who have fished this lake, trying to land Brown Beauty. They'll come back again and again—as long as the fish is alive. I've had my sport. I proved that Brown Beauty could be caught. Now I'm going to put the fish back before it dies so that some more fellows can have a chance to hook him."

"Well, I'll be jiggered," Pudge muttered. The others were too touched to say anything. They followed Ted down to the edge of the lake. Silently Ted untied the string that held the trout. He wet his hands, then eased Brown Beauty into the water. The fish lay there a moment, blowing its gills. Then suddenly Brown Beauty wiggled around, dived like a torpedo for deep water.

"Fish happy," Indian Jim said. That made Ted feel swell.

But Ted had something else on his mind. He said in a soft voice, "I'd like to see you alone, Mr. Jones."

Jeff Jones said, "Of course, Ted. Come into my office. As a matter of fact, I was going to ask you to come in anyway."

Ted followed the camp director into his private office. Once inside, Ted didn't waste time, "Sir, I want to talk to you about the old man over on the north side of the lake. He—well, you see, he isn't too well. He had an accident earlier in the summer and he's had quite a rough time of it. I was wondering if it would be all right if I brought him over here and took care of him during the rest of the camp period."

"This old man," the camp leader said thoughtfully. "What about him? How is it you know so much about his private life?"

Ted colored, but he said, without batting an eye, "I know all about him. You see, I've been seeing him regularly."

"You've been seeing him regularly. And all this, after I made you fellows promise not to go over there again?"

"Yes," Ted said quietly. "I've been seeing him be-cause—well, I can't explain it. Prospector is a funny old fellow. But he has a heart of gold and, if I might add, sir, it was Prospector who taught me the things that saved my life on the long hike back from the top of the peak. I knew you didn't want me to go over there, so I didn't say anything to you about going. I felt it was the simplest way out of the situation—without causing you any trouble, I mean. I had made up my mind that I was in the right and nothing you could have said would have stopped me."

"Coming from most fellows," the camp director said thoughtfully, "that would sound like outright revolt. However, I think I can see your point, Ted. You happen to be a very purposeful young man. You take your time in forming your opinions and then you are hard to swerve, once you set your mind to a thing."

"I'm glad you see it that way, sir."

"But," the camp director warned, "there is something else. Today you were ordered to fight fire. Under no condition were you to leave your post. In defiance of that order you left yours. I know, undoubtedly, that you went across the lake to where your friend was staying. But that was uncalled for. He could have taken care of himself. . . ."

Ted was about to protest that Prospector was beyond the point where he could aid himself. But he could see Jeff Jones' point. Jeff thought that if everyone left, just as Ted had, the fire would still be burning. In a sense, Jeff was right. So Ted said he was ready to take his punishment.

"I'll tell you your punishment tomorrow," Jeff promised.

17. CONCLUSION

TED slept that night because he was tired and because he had a clear conscience. The only thing that worried him was that Jeff Jones had refused to allow him to bring Prospector back. Of course, Prospector had recovered enough from the smoke to be able to get along by himself. But the man was old, and for some strange reason, Ted felt an affectionate attachment toward him.

The next morning, true to his promise, Jeff Jones decided on Ted's punishment. He said, "In view of the fact that you are so interested in the point awards, I am going to punish you where I think it will hurt the most. The track meet is scheduled for next Wednesday. I, therefore, must inform you that your name will not be accepted as an entry in the meet."

"I'm sorry, sir," Ted said. But he did not flinch. "As for something else, though, I think I had better tell you now. Until the camp period is over I plan to call on Prospector at least once a day. He's an old man and I'm worried about him."

"You're a strange fellow," the camp director said. "I'm punishing you for the very thing that you insist on doing again. But I'm not going to try to stop you. I'd much rather you told me than to have you sneak away, and then hear of it later. But I must warn you again—I know nothing of the old man. He may be crazy, as the rest of the fellows say. If anything should happen to you, I'm sure Colonel Cassiday would never forgive me."

Ted left, and because he had nothing different to do, he went down to the kitchen. There Charlie greeted him effusively. And when Ted asked for some canned goods, the Chinese cook gladly handed them to him. Ted, however, made one thing plain, "I'll pay you for this food. You can put the money in the kitchen budget."

He left the required amount of money, then got into his canoe and rowed across the lake. Prospector was better. He seemed glad to see Ted—until he saw the look on Ted's face.

"Say, youngster—you're down in the dumps. Now let me see. What could be wrong? Maybe this is it. Perhaps you've been punished for seeing me again after they told you not to."

Ted was evasive. "Oh, I wouldn't say that. . . ."

"You were never cut out to be a fibber," Prospector said. "I can see what you're thinkin'. Son, I can't tell you how sorry I am that you're in trouble on my account. But, by jingo, I can't tell you how happy I am that you wanted to do something for me. It makes an old man pretty happy, knowin' that someone thinks enough of him to help out when help's needed."

Ted began to smile again. "I don't know how you do it, but you have a way of making a fellow feel swell. I'm going to miss you, Prospector."

The old man said, "It's nice to hear you say that. Diggin' in these hills is gonna be lonesome without you. But enough o' that. I'm thankin' you for the food and things. I'll do my dratted best to repay you. There ain't much use of you stayin' around here the rest of the day. Summer's about over. If I was you, I'd get all the horseback ridin' and the swimmin' and the fishin' done you can get. You ain't gonna be here much longer."

Ted bade the old man good-by. He went back across the lake. It was odd how buoyed his spirit was. The thought of being barred from track competition did not worry him as he had thought it would. . . .

In the track meet, Rocky won two events and got second in another.

Ted went over, watched the camp director make the first and second place totals. They were, with the addition of the track points:

Rocky: 460   Ted: 330

The sight of the totals did something to Ted. He

said under his breath, "Come on, let's get out of here. For the next few days all I want to do is play. We'll swim, hike, ride—we'll do everything but stop to worry. How about it?"

Pudge followed him away. "Okay. But you're not fooling me a bit, Ted. I know what's eating you. It's the fact that you've lost out in the Gold Star Camper race. Well, I can't blame you much. You've had some bad breaks. And personally, I think you got an awful break when we went on that hike and I lost our flares and provisions."

"Let's forget it," Ted said, "It's over. Finished."

"No. It isn't over. Not yet. You're forgetting the one hundred and fifty points that will be awarded for doing the best deed of the camp period. You've still got a chance in that."

"A swell chance I've got," Ted said. "The only good deed I've done is to get into trouble with Jeff Jones. Besides, what about Rocky Stone? You know how he took command of that forest fire. The rangers said later that only his quick action prevented a possible catastrophe. And you have to hand it to Rocky on that score. He certainly proved his ability. He knew exactly what to do and he did it in as short a time as possible. No, that's the deed that will get the award. Both of us know that."

For once Pudge didn't argue with his pal. He knew

deep down in his own heart that Ted was speaking the truth.

Day after day passed by. The trees on the slopes were beginning to show a tint of brown as September approached. Snows were frequent on the high peaks. Word came through that there would be enough snow for the boys to get back to the railroad by sleigh—the same way they had come in.

Then the last day of camp arrived. The minute Ted got out of bed he remembered. "Oh, gosh," he said, "this is the day that Dad arrives. Pudge, how am I ever going to break the news to him?"

"I wish I knew," Pudge said. "He's counting on you. And I'm to blame. I kept blabbing in my letters how you were up there. I made it sound like you were a cinch to win. I'm sorry, Ted."

Ted's dad arrived shortly before noon. Their reunion was a joyful one. For long moments they stood there, pounding each other on the back, shouting and laughing. Then Ted sobered.

"Get set for it, Dad," he said. "I'm going to disappoint you."

"You mean the Gold Star Camper award is lost?"

"That's it," Ted admitted.

"Are you positive of it, son?"

"As positive as a man can be."

"Look up at me, Ted. That's it. Tell me this much.

Did you give everything you had? Did you fight with every bit of strength and courage you possessed?"

"I did, sir. I always do that."

Suddenly the elder Moran smiled. It wasn't an exuberant smile. Rather, it was a calm, thoughtful one. "That's good enough, Ted. When a man gives everything and then loses, the loss is no disgrace. And now that you've told me, let's forget it. I want to see the camp, of course. Show me around."

It was as simple as that. It proved to Ted that he had a remarkable father and it gave him a sense of pride he had never had before. The two Morans, accompanied by Pudge, visited points of interest. They returned in time for supper. Then after the evening meal, they all went into the lounge for the closing session of camp. Jeff Jones was presiding.

"Fellows," he said, "this is our last meeting. We've had a lot of fun here together and I feel that we've each learned a great deal. May I say to you that you could never come to a better place than the forest for a vacation? May I ask you to remember the lessons you have learned here throughout the rest of your life?

"Now I am not going to take up a lot of your time with a long speech. The idea right now is to get around to a thing that you have all waited three months to see —the awarding of Colonel Cassiday's great prize—the Gold Star Camper medal. I am pleased to tell you that

Colonel Cassiday is here tonight and will award the medal personally.

"But before I invite him up here, I want to comment upon the last part of the award. The race was very close all the way. Two men, however, predominated in the field. Every point has been accounted for except the last one hundred and fifty points to be given to the camper who performs the best deed of the camp period.

"In this connection I would like to talk about Rocky Stone. It has been my privilege to hear the praise of forest rangers for the way Rocky handled that fire. I feel sure that one of you boys left a spark in a campfire —a spark that started a fire that might have caused grave damage. But Rocky Stone through his heroic efforts brought credit to the camp for stopping the fire. I want to take this opportunity of paying special tribute to Rocky for this magnificent achievement."

Every boy in camp clapped loudly and for a long time.

"And now," Jeff Jones said, "I am going to turn the program over to the man who made this camp period possible. Will you come in, Colonel Cassiday?"

Slowly the outside door opened. Every eye was strained in that direction, awaiting a glimpse of the benefactor who had provided All-American Camp for the fellows. And then a man stepped inside. Ted Moran took one look and almost fainted.

"Prospector!" he muttered. For indeed the man was Prospector. And he was walking briskly up onto the platform. He was still bearded, still wearing tattered clothes. But in his hand was a safety razor and a little can of water. He mounted the platform.

"I came up this way, fellows," the old man said quietly, "because I wanted you to know for sure that I really am Colonel Cassiday. I realize that I owe you all an apology—and I'm going to make it as soon as I get these whiskers off."

The campers sat in stunned silence while Prospector —now Colonel Cassiday—hurriedly shaved off his beard. Then to their further surprise, he stepped out of his tattered clothes. Underneath he was wearing a business suit. The change was amazing. Now he looked like a distinguished business man—which he really was. His eyes were sharp and clear and his face, though bronzed, had a dignified, gentlemanly look. It was understandable why he had come in as he had—for no one would ever have believed him to be the old man who lived in the stone shack.

"I want to start at the beginning," he said. "You see, I never had a child of my own. My wife died when we were first married. I never married again. Later when I grew successful, I knew that there was one thing I would never be able to buy with money—that was the love of a son. So I decided to do the next best thing. I would devote a part of my money to something that a lot of young fellows would enjoy. That was how I got the idea of establishing this camp.

"Now mind you, I wanted to enjoy the camp myself. But I was afraid that if I came here and was recognized by you fellows, you would treat me as an idol or something. I didn't want that. I wanted to be near you where I could see you acting natural. I wanted to watch you having fun, without being known myself.

"Besides, a hobby of mine has always been collecting fossils and petrified things. That was why I was always digging. One day I had uncovered some particularly rich-looking specimens in front of my shack when a group of you fellows came up to see me. You were walking through the specimens and were smashing some of them. That was why I chased you away."

The old man suddenly smiled. "There was another reason, too. I knew that if you thought I was crazy, you would never connect me with being the real Colonel Cassiday. I don't blame you fellows for not coming back to see me. It was natural for you to stay away.

"Now there's one more thing I want to say. Jeff Jones did not even know where I was. I sent all my messages to the camp through a friend once a week. One week that friend was delayed and I was without food. But thanks to the thoughtfulness of one boy, Ted Moran, I didn't starve. Later when I was sick, that same boy took care of me, even though he knew that it was getting him in bad at the camp.

"That boy, Ted Moran, has earned my undying gratitude. He did the thing that he thought was right. He forgot his personal desires when he saw that he could be of some assistance to an old man. Not once did he question the fact that I was just an old man with not even enough to eat. Ted was not thinking of any personal reward. Rather, he was being kind because that is his nature.

"Now when I established this camp, I wanted to develop young men into real American citizens. I wanted to teach them that in this troubled world a man must learn to think of others as well as himself. I am proud that during this camp period at least one young man like that has turned up. I am sure that his example will make others of you into that same type of person.

"I pay tribute at this time also to Rocky Stone. His courage, too, was amazing. Next year he will be invited back to camp again. Perhaps he will win the Gold Star Camper award that he so narrowly missed this year. Now, if Ted Moran will come up?"

Dazedly, Ted Moran walked to the platform. The room was resounding with wild acclaim. Ted caught a look from his father. There was pride in his eyes. Ted smiled and his dad smiled back.

"Ted Moran," Colonel Cassiday said, "I present you with this beautiful gold star. In addition, I give you my personal check for fifty thousand dollars, which I authorize you to turn over to your father, who will give it to the authorities of your school. And now will you do me the honor of shaking my hand?"

There was a strange lump in Ted's throat as he took the old man's hand. "Thank you, Colonel Cassiday. . . ." Ted began.

"Prospector, Ted. It sounds more friendly."

"Prospector, then." Ted Moran grinned happily.